I0539884

As Above, So Below

Book One of the Augustino Case Files

Ryan Rennik

As Above, So Below (Book One of the Augustino Case Files) by Ryan Rennik
Trade paperback ISBN: 978-1-62898-001-1

Cover design: Alex Saskalidis

Copyright © Uncanny Books 2013

All rights reserved. No part of this publication may be reproduced, distributed, or transmitted in any form or by any means, including photocopying, recording, or other electronic or mechanical methods, without the prior written permission of the publisher, except in the case of brief quotations embodied in critical reviews and certain other noncommercial uses permitted by copyright law. For permission requests, write to the publisher, addressed "Attention: Permissions Coordinator," at the address below.

Uncanny Books
810 West Knox St.
Durham, NC 27701
http://uncannybooks.com/

This is a work of fiction. Names, characters, places, and incidents either are the product of the author's imagination or are used fictitiously, and any resemblance to any persons, living or dead, business establishments, events, or locales is entirely coincidental.

DEDICATION

For my wife: you are the love of my life

PROLOGUE

Roger Darnton had been having the same dream every night for the last month. It started out with just a few brief flashes of Gothic architecture, marble and bronze, statues and corridors. Some place he'd never seen before. Interspersed with darkness and shadows. Always with the creeping darkness blotting out the images he saw. And something shifting, twisting sinuously in the shadows that he could only sense out of the corner of his mind's eye. That was always there too, though he could never *quite* manage to see what it was.

In the dream, there was a sense of tension and foreboding, almost a kind of physical pressure pressing in all around him, as of gathering storm clouds that were soon to unleash their fury. But it wasn't just that indefinable sense of pressure. There was also anger, a fury that could not be appeased or satiated, like a feral child's, savage and unreasoning, seeking only to be expressed, and in the process, annihilate. There was a hunger too, a deep-seated need to take, and destroy and—especially—consume.

This presence, for that was how Roger thought of it, whatever it was, sought to compel him to find something. It whispered to him sometimes—if he were honest, Roger would be forced to admit that he now heard these whispers during his waking hours and it couldn't really even be described as a dream any more—though he couldn't understand the words it uttered. He knew that he had to take possession of something, some item, which he would find on someone or something else's behalf.

When Roger did what the voice, the presence wanted, there would

1

be pleasure. The presence made that abundantly clear. He would have more pleasure than he had ever experienced. It demonstrated this with a rapture better than any orgasm Roger had ever experienced running through his entire body. Roger was left shuddering and sweating and groaning when he finally came to on the dingy, faded carpet of his studio apartment. But if Roger were to turn away from the voice, if he were to dare shy away from doing its will, there would be pain. More pain than he had ever experienced. That, too, coursed through his body, like fire running along the nerves, melting his skin and flesh and bones and his very essence. That pain didn't end for a long, long while, an uncountable amount of time, even after he promised to obey. It was those nights that Roger woke up screaming.

He couldn't explain the dream—or whatever it was—to his girlfriend, Mary. He could barely even sleep, the adrenaline seemed to course through his veins almost continuously now. He would fall asleep as soon as his head hit the pillow, as though the dream summoned him. He would have the dream, the nightmare, whatever it was, which seemed to go on for hours. When he'd finally had all he could stand, and then some, he'd jerk awake, crying out and waking Mary. He would mumble an apology, then just lie there, replaying the dream, over and over again in his half-asleep, half-awake state. This had been happening every night for the last month. Until today. The dream had always been a little hazy, kind of fuzzy around the edges. Vague. Unclear. Not enough that you could quite put your finger on it. But today, in the wee hours of the morning, just before the first hints of false dawn, Roger had the dream again, and this time it all snapped into sharp focus. He knew what the dream wanted him to do.

Jesus, he thought. This can't go on. I've got to do something. Maybe I should just go and take a look, check it out. See if it's like it is in the dream. That can't hurt anything, can it?

That night, long after Mary had gone to sleep, Roger quietly slipped out of bed, dressed, and left home, heading to downtown Philadelphia to the Grand Lodge of Pennsylvania. Everyone knew where the place was: home of one of the country's oldest Masonic lodges, blah blah blah. Just home to a bunch of crazy old coots who liked to dress up in weird clothes and give each other secret handshakes. He had never been inside, taken the tour like the out-of-towners did. That was just for tourists. So why did he keep dreaming about this place? What was so special about it?

The front doors were huge, almost twenty feet tall. Roger knew they would be open and unlocked, just like in the dream, and they were. He stepped inside and was flanked by giant bronze sphinxes. The entry hall was enormous, running what looked like the entire length of the building. There were twin marble staircases that went up to the second floor. The building was built like a cathedral, parts of it a couple stories tall, but Roger knew that what he was looking for was down below, in the basement. Roger walked straight ahead, just like in the dream, and the staircase to the lower level was right where he knew it would be.

He walked down the staircase and immediately turned left. Roger ignored all the doors he passed, for he knew exactly where he was going, though he'd never been inside the building before. It really was just like the dream he'd been having, and Roger felt as though he were in the dream now.

Roger's feet made no sounds as he padded down the carpeted hallway. Reddish carpet with a gold design, built for lots of wear and tear, just like in a hotel, like one of those hotels where they hold wedding receptions, just like that place where his sister Susan's wedding reception had been held last— A blast of pain drove out Roger's idle thoughts, any thoughts at all. He submerged inside his own mind, then seemed to exit it altogether, floating up and behind his own body. Roger watched his body continue walking a little further, come to a door. His body paused for a moment, took a deep breath, then his hand reached out and turned the knob.

The room was mostly bare: some bookshelves on one wall, some framed pictures of old Masons on another, a glass case along a third wall, and two old guys—Masons, presumably—sitting in chairs shooting the breeze. They looked up as Roger opened the door, eyes wide, clearly not expecting anyone to enter the chamber and not knowing what was going on or why he was here.

"Who—who are you?" the older of the two guys said, not moving, his voice quivering. "What are you doing here? You're not supposed—"

Roger now knew why he had come here. The glass case along the wall, to Roger, now seemed to glow. It was there. The thing he sought. The man who had just spoken started to rise and Roger

3

shoved him as he walked past, hard, and the man and his chair tumbled to the floor.

Roger looked down into the case. There it was. He paused for a moment, savoring it, and felt a twinge of agony along his spine, then it was gone as quickly as it had arrived. He hastened to obey. Roger smashed open the glass case with his fist, not giving the glass a second thought and reached for the book. Click. What was that? He looked down and there was a piece of glass sticking out of the back of his hand. He instinctively plucked it out. It was razor sharp and there was blood. Roger's hand was starting to sting but it didn't matter, nothing mattered. He had the book! He had the book!

It took Roger a second, but he had heard a small sound behind him, and some instinct urged him to turn. The second man was standing there, pistol gripped tightly in one trembling hand.

Roger was far, far too close to achieving what he had come for to let some scared old man stop him now. He thought only of his promised reward as a chorus of a thousand unearthly voices swelled in triumph in his mind. Thoughts and fears were pushed aside, swept away by the tide of confidence that welled up in him. He gently placed the book back down on top of the case. Roger strode forward in two large steps, grabbed the man's hand in his, and twisted, back and upward, pulled the trigger, over and over again until the gun clicked empty.

The man's face and torso had been obliterated and Roger let him drop.

Roger was enraged that the Mason had dared to pull a gun on him. The other man was struggling to his feet, making bleating noises. Roger kicked him under the chin, neck snapping back. The man went sprawling. Roger walked over, stepped on his throat, crushed it, grinding it with his shoe into the carpet. He kept it there until the man was silent and unmoving.

Roger turned, walked back over to the case, picked it up—why was his hand hurting so badly?—and walked back through the Grand Lodge the way he had come.

Fuck! He had killed those two old dudes. Roger's heart was thumping out of control. He sat in his car a while, head back, eyes closed, fingers caressing the cover of that stupid book that he had stolen.

So now that he had the damn thing, why did he have the uncontrollable urge to get rid of it and give it to someone else?

CHAPTER 1

How do I get myself into these things?

I was running down an alley in Southeast Washington DC as fast as I could with the girl I had just rescued from a cult in tow. Shelley's former buddies—a group of freaks obsessed with death and immortality who called themselves the Bloodchildren—couldn't have been more than a block or so behind us. Shelley was drugged out of her mind and wearing four-inch platform combat boots, which wasn't exactly helping us make a quick getaway. We were making a beeline for my car, our breath turning to streamers of frost in the winter night air. The sidewalk was still covered by patches of ice from the snowfall we'd had a few days ago. Few things are uglier than the dirty snow piled up on DC streets after a winter storm. I had parked a few blocks away from the abandoned rowhouse the cult had been holed up in so I could sneak in to see what was what. I had managed to grab her from a back room upstairs while her new friends were involved in something weird, ritualistic, and extremely painful (from the sounds of it anyway) in the basement. The problem was, we made some noise exiting out the back—Shelley was still lukewarm about leaving with me—and now I was afraid they were almost on top of us.

To rewind just a bit, Shelley's father had hired me and my partner about two weeks prior. My partner, Jack Scanlon, had spoken with the father, but when Jack realized who the chick had fallen in with, he quickly passed off the case to me. Jack always lets me have the cases that involve being chased by insane goth kids. Nice guy. Oh well, I don't blame him, he's not getting any younger. I had to do all the legwork on the case, since Jack couldn't exactly infiltrate the local DC goth scene, being an old man with the appearance and attitudes of Archie Bunker. I didn't mind. To be honest, this case was pretty typical for us.

I was extremely wary of having the Bloodchildren catch up to Shelley and me as I panted and lugged her down an alley. Not that I thought they could beat the shit out of me—though I wouldn't be surprised if they could—but because of what I had seen them do in a goth/industrial club last week. When I had caught up with them at the club, a half dozen of them, evenly divided between men and women, were clustered around a little blonde girl barely old enough to legally get in. Perky tits and a fake ID usually works anyway. Now, I know for a fact that she was young because I had been ogling her before she got swarmed by the Bloodchildren and, well, I'd been feeling just a tad guilty about it. Look, I'm a red-blooded American male, still a pretty young guy and besides, she hadn't been wearing a shirt, just little black Xs of electrical tape over her nipples. How could I *not* have been staring at her ever since I first spotted her? Anyway, all I know is when she walked over to the Bloodchildren hovering in the corner, she looked like she was barely legal. When she stumbled away from them about five minutes later and fell down gracelessly in a corner, she looked like she was old enough to be a grandmother. A grandmother who'd had a hard life of raising ten screaming brats and breast-feeding them all until they were five— even the girl's cute little perky tits were sagging halfway down to her knees. I *knew* I had to Shelley away from them as fast as possible, if it wasn't already too late.

It took me a few days, but I tracked down the Bloodchildren to where they had set up shop in Southeast. It appeared that all the ones I had seen in the goth club, along with a few more I hadn't, were living in a shitty old rowhouse. I had kept the place under surveillance as best as I could for the past couple days trying to figure out their schedules, where they were keeping Shelley, etc. You know, all the usual investigative bullshit. From what I could tell, Shelley was there of her own free will. She left every now and then to get cigarettes or booze or pizza or whatever with one or two of the Bloodchildren and always came back. She didn't look great or incredibly happy to be there, but then again it was hard to tell under the wild hair, white face makeup, and layers of black shrouding. They were certainly letting her have relatively free run of the place, and she wasn't obviously trying to escape from them. Neither did she look old and withered yet like the club girl.

I have no idea what they ultimately had in mind for Shelley. Maybe they were going to use her as a snack later on. Maybe they were eventually going to initiate her into the club. Not sure. Either way, it was a pretty ugly fate for a young girl. In any case, Jack and I were being paid a sizable amount of money to bring her back home, and I'd rather not see a young girl get caught up in all that anyway, so I was going to do whatever it took to get her out of there.

Back to the present: I had just turned around to see if I could spot any of the Bloodchildren following us. I had one hand clamped tightly on Shelley's arm so she couldn't get away from me. I caught movement ahead out of the corner of my eye. One of the Bloodchildren had just popped up from around the corner, not five feet away.

I could feel my heart in my throat. How the hell did he get in front of us? I was sure I had seen the guy go into the house a few hours ago and not come out since then. He snarled and raised his hands, but there was no way in hell I was going to let him do to me whatever it was they had done to that girl in the club. My right foot went straight up into his balls. He doubled over and dropped to his knees, not even making a sound. I clouted him in the back of the head with my free hand as we brushed past. I just hoped that none of his friends had heard any of that. I gave him a quick look as we rounded the corner—yep, he was still down and not moving—and continued to head toward my car, which was only a block or two away.

I honestly thought we were in the clear. Maybe I'm a hopeless, naive optimist. Maybe I was just plain desperate. I don't know. My car was just around the next corner. As I continued dragging Shelley with me, I saw that there were two Bloodchildren leaning against my car with their arms crossed and extremely self-satisfied smirks on their faces. Fuck. They weren't going to make this easy on me. One of them, the guy with the spiky black Peter Murphy hair I had seen before, uncrossed his arms and started walking toward me, still grinning. I suspected he was their leader, but it was hard to tell. They seemed to be a pretty egalitarian pack of youth-sucking vampires. The second one, a woman with a shaved head and chains all over, kept back a little and let Peter Murphy take the lead.

I let Shelley drop to the ground. Dead weight. She was still drugged up and mostly incoherent. Shelley was just going to have to take care of herself for a minute or two while I saved both our asses. The male Bloodchild took a couple more steps toward me and *pounced*. Jesus, he was fast. He went for my face, trying to thrust his black nail polish-covered thumbnails into my eye sockets. I twisted away, protecting my eyes, and landed a couple good punches to his gut. I barreled into him, locking him down and wrapping my arms around him. He stunk like rotting meat under the scent of his cheap cologne and the beer and cigarettes on his breath. I tried to punch him in the kidneys, but he wormed away and shoved me back. I'm no small guy either. Damn, he was a lot stronger than he looked. Must be those centuries of clean living. I stumbled over Shelley just a bit, or maybe it was a patch of ice, but I lost my balance for a second, and then he was on top of me. I twisted around, getting him under me and flat on his back on the sidewalk. I poured punch after punch into his face, ripping my knuckles open on his sharp little yellow teeth. His breath was like roadkill as he panted into my face. By this point, though, his face was covered in blood and the fight had gone out of him.

The female Bloodchild had apparently been getting herself worked up into a frenzy—guess she didn't like the treatment her boyfriend had received—and came at me with her arms flailing wildly. I ducked a little and came up inside her guard and popped her one across the jaw. Guess chivalry really is dead. The yelling stopped, which was nice, and her head hit the pavement pretty hard. I resisted the urge to give her a couple kicks to the face. See: I can be a gentleman when I want to be.

Shit, not much time now, I knew the others would have heard all that racket. I grabbed Shelley, helped her stumble to her feet, and propelled her into the car by main force. I ran around to the driver's side, got it started, and peeled out. Didn't see any other Bloodchildren in the rear view mirror either, which suited me just fine, just a homeless guy in the street, staring at us with his mouth open.

I called Shelley's father on my cell phone as soon as we made it back to Constitution Avenue and I could see the Capitol Building.

My heart rate had pretty much calmed down almost to a normal level at that point. I wanted nothing more than to get her back to her family, get paid, and get home. Dad sounded almost embarrassingly grateful on the phone, and we arranged to meet in Rosslyn, just over the Key Bridge in Virginia in a half hour. Virginia has never been to my liking, and I don't head into the wilds of Virginia more than one or twice a year if I can help it. Over the last few years, it's become the land of strip malls, luxury condos, and over-priced *tapas* bars. No thanks. Not my scene.

I parked near the Rosslyn Metro station—that's the DC subway system, to you out-of-towners—and waited, still shaking a little. The girl was starting to come around and make slightly more coherent noises.

"So what the hell were you thinking, wanting to join those freaks?" I've never won any awards for tact or sensitivity, but it was an honest question.

She wasn't completely lucid yet. I handed her a half-empty soda bottle I had been working on earlier and she polished it off. "Don't . . . want to . . . get old . . . like my . . . parents. Want to . . . live . . . forever." Talking and thinking were still clearly a struggle for her. Well, I can't blame her for not wanting to get old, I guess. Turning thirty had been a bitch for me, and I'll be the first one to admit that it sure as shit sucks when the metabolism slows and you start to get pudgy and slow. But I'll be goddamned if I'm willing to suck the youth right out of club kids every night just so I can stay spry. I'm more than willing to suck down a Slimfast or hit the gym. Hell, I'll even pop the occasional Viagra when the time comes.

"They were . . . pretty cool to start off with. Didn't know . . . what they were at first."

"You and me both, Shelley."

"They told me . . . they had picked me out special. They said . . . if I joined them . . . I could be just like them . . . and live forever. They were . . . nice to me. Treated me right. Did you . . . kill them . . . back there? I heard . . . yelling and screaming. What *was* that?"

I sighed a bit. "No, that was probably *me* you heard yelling and screaming. Look, Shelley, I saw what they did to a girl at a club last week. She started out twenty-one and ended up looking like a little old lady. Did you know that? Did you know they did that to people?"

She didn't answer, and wouldn't look me in the eyes, which I took to mean 'yes.' After a little while, Shelley started crying. I didn't press her on it. I knew she had been through enough. At least I had gotten her out before she joined them; to my knowledge, she hadn't yet participated in any of their life-sucking escapades. I gave her a couple napkins out of yesterday's McDonald's combo meal bag. Private detectives tend to eat like shit, I've found, but that's just part of the job.

We waited in silence until her dad arrived ten minutes later—what else was I going to say to her? They shared a big hug, and I got a fat envelope with what looked like a decent size bonus, so I guess everyone was happy. After Shelley's dad bundled her into his car, I warned him to get her far, far away from DC before she ended up either dead or back with them. He mumbled something about taking her to visit her grandmother in California for a while, and I guess that would have to do. At least the Bloodchildren probably wouldn't be able to get their claws back into her in sunny California.

I headed back into DC to hit the office quickly before going home for some well-deserved R&R. All in a night's work.

CHAPTER 2

I rolled up to my office, parked on a side street, put the Club on the steering wheel, and walked over to unlock the front door of the building. On the way, I waved to Ollie, an old black guy, semi-homeless, who keeps an eye on Jack's and my cars for us. We give him five or ten bucks a week. Was it extortion? Insurance? I was never sure, never really cared, since nothing ever happened to my car.

Our office is in the more "transitional" part of U Street. Jack and I work in a dump, but at least it gives us a place to meet clients and store files. Besides, some of our more upscale clientele seem to almost enjoy coming to a rundown office with dim lighting in a part of town that hasn't been thoroughly "gentrified" yet. Once the gentrification finally comes, we probably won't be able to afford the rent anymore, but that's a ways off.

There was a small wrapped package propped up against the inner door to the office of Scanlon and Augustino, Private Investigators. I'm half of that partnership, by the way: Michael Augustino. Thirty-one, tall, dark, and handsome (you knew I'd say that). Well, I'm about six feet tall anyway, both my parents were Sicilian, and I have no problem getting laid when I make the effort, though that's pretty seldom these days. Given up on all that, after . . . well, *after*. I'm a Washingtonian, born and bred, and I've been a private detective most of my adult life. I've been partnered with Jack the whole time and he's taught me pretty much everything I know about investigation. Business is going well, life in general is going pretty well, though the love life is currently non-existent. Those are the high points.

Anyway, opening the package, I found a thin hardback book—*Atlas Shrugged* by Ayn Rand—and a handwritten note on fancy parchment. It read, "Dear Michael, I hope this finds you well. I know those little Bloodchildren can be a bore." That was the understatement of the millennium. "In any case, please drop by as soon as possible. I could use your assistance in locating something important. It shouldn't be too difficult for a man of your talents, but time is of the essence in this important matter. Best regards, The Bookworm. P.S. Why don't you read the book some time, you just might learn something." That Bookworm is a very funny guy. Maybe a little too nosy—how did he know about the Bloodchildren case?—but he's a good guy, and a very good client. But what was the deal with the book? Did he want me to carry the weight of the world on my shoulders for him? I opened the book, flipped through it, noticed that it was an autographed first edition. The Bookworm knew my weakness for books and exploited it at every turn. I groaned a bit because I was much more interested in heading home and hitting the sack than I was in starting a new case. But his note made it sound like this was an important one, and important cases mean big fees. Big fees mean, well, Jack and I don't have to worry about paying rent for a while.

I unlocked the office, went inside, and sat down at my desk, staring around the room almost in a daze. I washed out my nicks and cuts as best I could in our little half bathroom, put some band-aids on the cuts, got some ice out of the mini-fridge and tried to get the swelling on my shredded knuckles to go down. That Bloodchild had some sharp, nasty little teeth. Hope I didn't need a rabies shot. I called Jack at home even though it was after one in the morning. I knew he'd still be up doing whatever it is that Jack does at home. Drink heavily, eat take-out, watch TV, and look at porn, I suspected.

"Talk to me," I heard his gruff voice say after four rings. I could tell he was half in the bag.

"Well, I got the girl back to her father, and we got paid. A bonus even."

"Ah, good boy." I could hear him grinning. "How ugly was it?"

"Let's just say that I don't want anything more to do with goth kids for a very long time. And my right hand hurts like hell. I think I'm going to go plunge it into a bucket of ice." I always like using guilt trips on Jack whenever I think he's not pulling his share of the load. Not that they ever seem to have an effect on him. He says his ex-wife immunized him against them. She was a real guilt-trip pro from the sounds of it; I can't even compete.

"I'm sure you did great, kid. Don't even need old Jack anymore, do you? You should hit the hay, buddy. Come in late tomorrow, have a good night's sleep, you'll feel like a new man."

"No can do, Jack, we've got a new case from the Bookworm. I need to head over there first thing tomorrow morning. He dropped off a note here for me—"

"Ah, shit, you go tell that fucker that—"

"No, no, it's OK, Jack, I don't mind. He's not such a bad guy and he pays well. You know that. We can use the money."

The Bookworm is a rich weirdo we occasionally work for. For some reason he and my partner have never gotten along well together. I gather there's some sort of history between them, but the one time I asked Jack about it, he got unusually tight-lipped, so I didn't press him on it. Our work for the Bookworm isn't anything too exciting, usually just tracking down something or someone for him, or accompanying him while he goes to meet with some shady character to buy a book. He pays well enough, and he had seemed to have taken a shine to me, especially since he knows I'm a bibliophile myself, so I don't mind doing his scutwork. We booklovers have to stick together.

"Whatever. Just take care of yourself. Don't wear yourself out running his errands."

"I'll be fine, Jack. I'm going to head home now. There's nothing else going on here at the office." We said our good-byes. I knew Jack would probably have another drink and pass out. I left, locking up. Man, that pillow sure was going to feel good. Then I remembered the nightmares I've been having every night for the last week. All doom, gloom, and terror. Waking up with night sweats and screaming every night sure takes some of the fun out of getting a little well-deserved shut-eye. Sometimes life isn't all it's cracked up to be.

CHAPTER 3

The scream made me sit bolt upright in my bed. Then I realized it was me screaming. Again. I was drenched in flop sweat, as were my sheets and pillowcase. I couldn't remember exactly what my nightmare had been, except that it left me with a sense of foreboding and doom. I vaguely remembered running down an endless corridor lined with books, while being chased and harried by something behind me that was going to consume me when it caught up. That's a hell of a way to begin a new day.

Damn it, I used to consider sleep a hobby. I love nothing more than catnaps and that peaceful sensation you get as you start to drift off to sleep. Now I couldn't even enjoy that lately, knowing I was going to wake up terrified with my heart pounding out of my chest. Surely the Bloodchildren hadn't gotten to me that badly, had they? It was pretty horrific seeing what they had done to that girl in the club, but as far as I knew, I had gotten away from them cleanly. They were old news. Shelley was back with her (presumably) loving parents and the Bloodchildren didn't even know my name. It had to be something else.

I eventually said to hell with it and struggled out of bed around nine o'clock after failing to fall back asleep. I wolfed down a quick breakfast and got ready to meet the Bookworm. I walked outside and hopped in my Fiero. Yeah, I know, it's a piece of shit and I've had it for probably ten or eleven years, but it's the only car I've ever owned. I saved for six months to buy it. My buddy George helped me get it fixed up, and it's been reliable ever since. Yep, I love that

GT. The fact that I got my first blowjob in it probably has a little something to do with that. (I can see you doing the math in your head. Yeah, I was a bit of a late bloomer. I make no apologies. I was saving myself for marriage. OK, you don't believe that? The truth is, I was shy around girls, until I realized they wanted to have sex as much as I did. The rest is history.)

I drove over to the Bookworm's house tucked away in a quiet little neighborhood in the Glover Park area of Northwest, enjoying the day. Traffic was light—I guess most people were already at work—and I made my way over to his house and parked in the driveway. What a great little neighborhood tucked away in DC. If I could afford it, I'd love a house here. Never happen on my salary though. Lots of trees, quiet all the time, no crime. Man, if only the local housewives knew their quiet neighbor was a sorcerer.

I was greeted at the door by a young woman who works for the Bookworm. She's lanky with long, greasy red hair. Not all that pretty, just a plain girl who never wears make-up and won't look me in the eye. She rarely says more than two sentences to me, but I always smile at her and try to get her to laugh. Haven't succeeded yet. She reads his books to him and helps him work magic, so he calls her "The Lector." Gotta love these sorcerer-types with their nicknames. All of them are afraid to use their True Names because it could be used against them. Me, I couldn't care less. Everyone in the business knows my name is Michael Augustino, though mostly everyone just calls me Augustino. Not that I'm a sorcerer myself. I'd just as soon not have anything to do with it, but Jack and I seem to attract all the local magical freaks. Hey, their money still spends, and every last one of them has more dollars than sense. (I kill me.)

The Lector unlocked the door and beckoned me inside. I gave her my patented grin. (My "hey sexy" one, not my "I just shat on your porch" one.) No response; no surprise there. Maybe next time.

She ushered me into the Bookworm's Library. I loved this room. Huge, open space. Absolutely covered, floor to ceiling, with built-in bookshelves. He had a big Oriental rug covering the floor, an Old World globe in a floor stand, one of those gigantic old desks that weighs half a ton, and a couple of enormous overstuffed brown leather chairs. (Note to self: never volunteer to help the Bookworm move.) I was gazing around the room just staring at all the books, like I always did, when the Bookworm cleared his throat. He was sitting behind his desk with a little smile on his face. "I always enjoy your reaction to my Library."

The Bookworm is a tall, skinny, middle-aged guy with salt-and-pepper hair and goatee. He kind of shuffles along rather than actually walks, and the sleeves on shirts are always too short. I can't criticize him too much, his money is just as green as anybody else's, and his taste in books is impeccable. Most rich dudes are eccentric as hell anyway, in my experience, and the Bookworm is far more normal than some I've come across. I've always liked the guy, but I sense that there is a lot more to him than meets the eye. He's clearly got a lot of money, he's well-connected in our local little occult subculture, and he's obsessed with books. Not that being obsessed with books is a bad thing; I've been accused of that once or twice myself. My little collection is nothing compared with the Bookworm's treasures, though. Plus, I suspect that he's made more than a few enemies over the years, based on some hints that he's dropped, and some things he's had me do for him. He's a cryptic guy, but one of these days I'll figure him out.

"Have a seat, Michael. 'Take a load off,' as they say. It's early yet and from the looks of it, I suspect that you had a late night last night."

"Did my good deed for the year last night." I plopped down.

"Why, Michael, you're not getting soft in your old age, are you?" he said with a smile. "May I offer you any refreshments? Coffee?" I shook my head no. I don't drink coffee, and I would just as soon he cut to the chase. I *was* still dragging a little from last night's exertions, and I have to admit, I was more than a little curious about what he wanted.

"Very well then. I am looking for a book."

"No shit." He's always looking for one damn book or another.

"A very special book."

"Aren't they all?"

"I think you're just the man to help me locate it. I'll pay you twenty thousand dollars for the book, along with whatever expenses you incur while acquiring it."

"Twenty grand? What's the catch? That's *considerably* more than you've ever paid before, by a huge margin. Why so much?"

"Well . . . I'm not the only person interested in acquiring this book." Ah, the truth starts to come out. "There are likely to be some very determined people who would also like this book. I know it entered Washington, DC yesterday afternoon; my scrying has revealed that much. The book itself is shielded though, either by whoever has possession of it currently or through its own properties, so I don't know the exact location of the book. That's why I need your help: the Lector and I can't simply waltz over to whoever has it right now and persuade them to give it to us. I need *you* to find it for me. I will know if the book leaves DC, and I'll let you know if I sense that happening, but I can't tell you exactly where it is right now or who has it. I can only leave it to your considerable investigative skills to locate it. It's a valuable book, and I would suspect that whoever has it has at least some knowledge of its occult importance."

I had to take him on his word that the book was currently in DC. I had watched the Bookworm scry before. Pretty neat stuff—though all magic, in my experience, is inherently creepy. Makes the hair on my arms and back of my neck stand on end, and I always feel like I'm struggling with the fight or flight instinct when I'm around it. The last time I saw the Bookworm scry, he took out a dictionary, went into a trance, flipped to a random page, and started underlining words in what seemed to be random order. When we strung the words together in order after he got out of the trance, he had the answer to his question. Needless to say, I was a little creeped out and a lot impressed.

"So what's the book? And don't be coy, Bookworm. I'll need as much info on it as you can give me. The more info you can give me, the faster I'll have the book in your greedy little hands." This ought to be good.

"Well," he said almost reluctantly, "it is a book from the private collection of Benjamin Franklin. A one of a kind piece. Until very recently, the book was held in a private collection in the Philadelphia area. I've had my eye on it for years, but there was no way I could acquire it from its previous owner. For some reason unknown to me, someone has removed it from its previous location and brought it down to Washington. I believe that the book's previous owner is not aware of this. I have no idea what the current possessor intends to do with the book, but I assume the book will either be sold, or it will enter a private collection here in DC. It might even enter the Smithsonian's collection, or the Library of Congress." He shuddered at that thought. "In any case, I want to gain possession of the book before any of that can happen."

"What do you mean you don't know what the current possessor of the book will *do* with it? It's a book. You read it, put it on the shelf, admire it every now and then—right? Sure, the book has got to be unbelievably valuable, but what's the draw? What did you mean when you were talking about someone *doing* something with it?"

"Well . . . this book is not exactly one of the typical antiquarian books I've had you procure for me in the past. This is a very special book. And by that, I mean that it's a book dealing with magic. A very peculiar and dark form of magic." I was not liking the sound of this. The hairs on the back of my neck were very seriously considering standing up.

"I believe that someone with the proper knowledge of the occult could use the book to pierce a boundary between our world and some other form or level of existence. That person could then contact an entity that resides in that other world. This entity has been called Tiamat in past ages. The Sumerians and the Babylonians knew of it as a god/demon responsible for great evil. It may have even been somehow responsible for their civilizations' downfalls. This entity has always sought to enter our world, and is willing to offer almost anything to someone capable of fulfilling that desire. I believe that Benjamin Franklin, and his fellow Freemasons, were able to compile enough esoteric knowledge to make this feat possible. In fact, I believe they laid out a sorcerous ritual that is a blueprint for doing just that. *That's* what I believe is in this book. I don't know what Franklin and his contemporaries had intended to do with their knowledge. Perhaps they had enough scruples not to actually employ the ritual, but whoever acquires the book might not be so reluctant."

I caught myself groaning softly. The Bookworm continued relentlessly.

"The book is bound in a dark leather. Possibly human leather. Embossed on the cover are several traditional Masonic symbols—a square, a compass, a large letter 'G'—that sort of thing. These symbols may or may not be gilded. The spine is bare. On the title page are the words "The Thirty-third Esoteric Key of the Invisible Lodge." The author is listed as Benjamin Franklin himself. The book is written in fairly archaic English, as you might expect, and it's almost certainly written in an archaic, technical style. I believe it would be largely incomprehensible to a layman. Someone who understands the principles of magic would be able to decipher it with a little work, though. The ritual itself is purportedly very straightforward. After all, Tiamat would not want to make it difficult for someone interested and able to contact it. The book will have a number of diagrams and line drawings, especially as it goes along, to illustrate exactly how Tiamat is to be contacted."

My conscience required me to interject a few questions. "So what exactly are *you* planning on doing with the book, Bookworm? I mean, I can see that it's probably not a good idea for most of the freaks in this town to get their hands on a book like this. I certainly wouldn't want any of our elected officials to; but, other than the money, why should I go out and find the book and give it to you? As nice of a guy as you are, I don't know that I'd consider it a good thing if you were to contact Laundromat or whatever it is and make a bargain of your own."

He paused. Long silence while he looked down at his chest. "I am going to do something with this book that I have never done before. This . . . this is not something I will do lightly. I want you to know that. I truly, deeply love books."

"But . . . I am going to destroy the book." I was, well, shocked doesn't begin to cut it, and I looked over at the Lector in disbelief. She couldn't even look at me.

"I haven't always been the best person in the world, but I'm not the kind of man who would bargain away my soul, and possibly the entire world, just to gain power. I already *have* power. I simply can't take the chance that whoever acquires the book might actually use it. The book *has* to be destroyed."

The Bookworm was staring into my eyes. He could probably see the skepticism on my face. "Besides, if I was going to use the book for harmful or selfish purposes, wouldn't I have made up some innocuous story about what the book was and why I wanted it? I have chosen to be brutally honest with you. I mean no offense to you, Michael, but I don't believe your level of magical knowledge would allow you to discern exactly what the book can allow an educated reader to do. The most important reason why I contacted you in this matter is because you are one of the few people I trust enough to do the right thing and hand the book over to me to be destroyed, rather than using it yourself or selling it to someone else."

I believed him. I was oddly touched in a way. I've always considered myself a pretty decent judge of character, and for better or for worse, I was sure he was telling me the truth, even though the idea of him ever destroying any book—especially one with this much history and mojo—was hard to swallow.

There was clearly a lot more to this story than meets the eye. The hairs on the back of my neck had finally decided to start standing up. Never a good sign. I've never been a bleeding heart, but I do have a conscience. I had to at least try to stop some of the freakshows around town from getting the book. Besides: there was still the twenty grand in it for me and Jack. I could come up with a way to spend that much money in five minutes.

"OK, Bookworm, I'll do it on one condition," I said without a great deal of enthusiasm. "You have to let me watch you destroy the book."

"Excellent! I agree to your condition." I didn't like that twinkle in his eye one bit. "I knew I could count on you, Michael. I wish I could give you more of a head start on this one, but unfortunately I don't know any more than I've already told you. You have my number, so call or stop by when you have any updates and let me know how your search is progressing. This is an important one, Michael. I have every confidence in you."

I took my leave of him and the Lector showed me out. Still no smile from her. I wondered what her opinion on the whole matter was, but I knew she'd never give it to me straight. I've never once heard her say a word against the Bookworm, and their exact relationship was always a bit unclear to me. Sure, he was the master and she the apprentice, but he wasn't more than ten years older than her, and she probably cleaned up all right . . . .

I had some ideas where the book might be, or at least a couple people who might be able to give me leads. I headed out to the car, wondering who I should start with.

Just before I got into the car, the Bookworm opened his front door and stepped out briefly. "Oh, and Michael? Be careful." The hairs were standing up on the back of neck now—and I don't think the sudden chill was due to the winter weather.

CHAPTER 4

Having been born and raised in DC, I've watched Chinatown dwindle to a mere shadow of its former self. Just a couple blocks wide and not many more long, it's now little more than a string of take-out joints being slowly encroached upon by upscale chain restaurants, bars, and office buildings. I'm not even sure how many ethnic Chinese even live there anymore. Couldn't be all that many left. But Po Wen and Po Zhi still live there, and they're the ones I wanted to see. If anyone in town would know about a new occult tome in town, one of them would. They're brothers, rivals, alchemists, and brokers of information pertaining to weirdness and all things magic. Not much happens in the scummier parts of DC that one or both of them doesn't know about. I decided to try Po Wen, the eldest, first. That seemed the respectable thing to do. Plus it helps that Po Wen owed me a favor for past services rendered, so I figured this was as good a time to call that in as any.

Parking took about twenty minutes, and required a five block walk to get to where Po Wen sees clients. Even so, I had to park at a broken meter and risk a parking ticket from one of the ubiquitous meter maids trolling for her next victim. I walked into the Szechuan Jade Garden #1 restaurant and was greeted by the little old Chinese lady who works as the hostess/manager who immediately thrust a menu into my hands. "I'm here to see Po Wen," I said quietly, not wanting the tourists and office workers having an early lunch to overhear me. Her semi-smile froze. She snatched the menu back, turned, and headed upstairs. I assumed she wanted me to follow, so

I trotted off after her. The staircase to the upper floor was narrow, and as we walked up it, I wondered if this would be the time it finally collapsed, as I always did. The stairs creaked and groaned, but oddly enough I didn't plunge to my doom. She seated me at a booth in the upstairs dining room, where there were no other customers. "You wait," she said, and walked into the back room. After a few minutes, a waiter wearing a stained tuxedo brought me a bowl of hot and sour soup with a plate of wontons. The soup was absolutely delicious, though the wontons were stuffed with what may have been dog food. I knew what not to order next time. I had just finished the soup when the old lady reappeared. "You come." She walked into the back room again, this time with me following. We walked down a long, dimly lit corridor past a bunch of shut doorways. Every time I came here I wonder what was behind them. Alas, guys like Po Wen rarely welcome inquiries about their personal affairs. Probably just where they keep the stacks of dog carcasses for the entrees anyway.

She knocked a couple times on the door to his office, then opened the door and practically pushed me inside. I heard the door click shut behind me.

"Augustino! Hello, my friend. How you doing?" Po Wen was wedged into the area behind his desk. The room was small and cramped and reeked of old man and various indescribable smells, all competing to blow out my sinuses. Po Wen is probably about sixty, but he could be anywhere from forty to a hundred and sixty for all I know. Jack introduced me to Po Wen and his younger brother Po Zhi years ago. Jack had warned me that while the brothers were the best in the business, their information always came with a price. Po Wen and I have always had a cordial relationship, and we frequently trade my services and legwork for his information. It's always been a satisfying business relationship for both us, I think, since we both usually end up getting what we want.

We chitchatted for a while about weather, and crime, and absolutely nothing important for probably twenty minutes. Po Wen required the small talk, I had learned. The first time I met him without Jack being present, he got very offended that I wanted to get right down to business as soon as I came in. I learned my lesson and let him dictate the pace of our conversation. When it became clear that he was ready to talk business, I mentioned almost off-handedly that I was interested in locating a particular book.

"It's one that would have just arrived in town, within the last day or two, I think. Someone would have brought it down from Philly. They're probably looking to find a buyer for the book here in DC. I've heard that the original owner or author was Benjamin Franklin." I didn't want to reveal too much about what was inside the book. Hell, for all I know, Po Wen didn't know who good ol' Ben was anyway. There was no point in making any more of this public knowledge than it already was. While Po Wen and I had a good business relationship, I had no doubt that he would sell me out to a higher bidder, or go after the book himself, if he knew how important it might be. It would be "just business," and I'm sure he'd expect me to grin and bear it.

He mumbled a bit and wouldn't look me in the eye. Why would he be reticent to talk about the book? "I fully understand that you might not be able to assist me, Po Wen. The book is valuable, and it's important to me to find it, but I know that even your insight doesn't touch all corners of the city. I wonder if possibly Po Zhi might have learned of the book's location or seller?" I really hoped I wouldn't have to go to his brother. Po Zhi is, to put it politely, a dick. Rude, obnoxious, aggressive, and miserly. Unfortunately, sometimes Po Zhi was simply a better source of information than his elder brother. It really just depended on what you were looking for. We both knew that I could be at Po Zhi's office in the back of a massage parlor around the corner in ten minutes, so it was a believable, if veiled, threat. No need to piss him off, but I needed Po Wen to understand that I had other alternatives.

"I see," he said, starting to look a little peeved. I didn't want to piss him off and make him shut down, but I didn't want him to think he could jerk me around or jack the price up beyond what I thought was reasonable if he knew something. I had done him a favor a couple months ago and felt that was enough payment for the location of the book. I just had to hope he felt the same.

I let him sit and stew for a minute, neutral expression on my face and looking vaguely around the room. Not that I could read any of the Chinese writing on the papers he had scattered all around. Po Wen seemed to reach some kind of decision and began making a weird little whistling noise. What the hell? Had he finally gone over the deep end? Too much opium? There were some rustling noises in a corner of the room I couldn't see from where I was sitting. It sounded like rats mating. It continued for a minute, then a little *thing* crawled up onto Po Wen's lap, then onto his shoulder. It looked like a cross between a naked rat and a little Chinese man four or five inches tall.

"Jesus!" I jumped back, almost upsetting my chair.

"No, no, my friend, it's all right," he said, waving one hand at me. No it's not, there's a thing on your shoulder... "This is just one of my little pets, he learns things, sees things for me, goes places I cannot. He may know of your book. We will ask him and see what he knows."

Dear God, it was looking at me with those beady little rat eyes and whispering in Po Wen's ear. Is this how he finds out what's going on all over the city? I had figured he had a crystal ball or paid off homeless people or something. I really didn't want to think about it. I was getting mildly nauseous and couldn't look at that thing anymore. I had to look away and try my damnedest to think happy thoughts. I'm not very good at that under the best of conditions.

They whispered sweet nothings in Chinese to each other for a while. "I would suggest that you try the Flea Market tonight. Whoever has the book now will likely be there. I'm sorry that I can't tell you any more. Even my little friends," he stroked the thing's head and cooed at it, it seemed to eat up the attention, "don't know everything. Perhaps if you came back in a day or two, I might know more."

I thanked Po Wen and told him that I would indeed check out the Flea Market and come back in a couple days if the lead didn't pan out. Oh well, if I had to go to the Flea Market, I had to. No two ways about it. But damn it all, the freaks sure do come out for the Flea Market. I was more than ready to get away from the little darling perched on Po Wen's shoulder, so I made my farewells a little quicker than I usually do and got out the hell out of Dodge.

CHAPTER 5

The Flea Market isn't a typical flea market, filled with tables of old glassware and cheap sunglasses and records that no one wants anymore. For one thing, it's held every full moon in a warehouse in the worst part of South Capitol Street down in Southeast. It's been a staple of the DC underground for decades, and is currently being run by a guy who calls himself Lupo (yeah, I know, never trust a guy who goes by the name Lupo) who obviously had the whole obsession with wolves, the full moon, etc. going. At least I assume he's the owner of the panel van with a big airbrushed image of a wolf baying at the moon that's always parked there. The Flea Market is basically a gathering place for all the local mystics and occultists to get together and exchange junk, gossip, tricks of the trade, that sort of thing. Most of the items offered for sale are honest-to-God junk, just as with any flea market, but occasionally someone shows up with the good stuff, and that's what keeps people coming back. Even *I've* been impressed with a few of the things I've seen for sale there. I've never thought much of the place, but Jack absolutely loves it. He's dragged me there more times than I care to remember. He's a sucker for any trinket someone claims is magical. He probably carries around a dozen or more good luck charms, mojo bags, "mystic artifacts," what have you. I have my doubts about all of them, but I keep that to myself. Jack takes his trinkets very seriously, and he'll tell anyone who cares to listen how this piece or that saved his life years ago or brought him good fortune during the Nixon administration or something.

The Flea Market usually doesn't start until about nine p.m. or so, and the first hour or two is usually fairly dead, just like most DC nightclubs, oddly enough. Hell, let's face it, the Flea Market is as much a social event as anything else. I had plenty of time to kill, so I decided to drop by the office and see what Jack was up to.

I found Jack in the office staring at the computer and pretending to shuffle papers around as he heard me come in. Jack is, well, kind of dumpy looking. Medium height, with a growing pot belly that slumped over his belt. Slovenly; Jack is one of those guys who can never managed to keep his entire shirt tucked in. He usually wears some of his lunch too. I will say this for him, though: for a guy in his early sixties, he had a full head of hair—mostly still black too.

"Hey, kid, how's it going? Come here and take a look at the tits on this one!" Oh God, he was porn surfing again. Just when I had finally gotten all the viruses and spyware cleaned off his computer. Jack was computer-illiterate for the most part, and I was always having to fix his office computer or show him how to copy and paste, but I've never minded helping Jack out. Most of his computer problems stemmed from all the porn that he looked at on the Internet. That computer was a magnet for viruses and spyware. I walked over and feigned interest in the nude pictures for a while—I had no intention of asking Jack why the chick was wearing clown make-up—before plopping myself down at my desk and telling him about the Bookworm's case, my meeting with Po Wen, and my plans to attend the Flea Market that evening.

"Ah, that explains it then," Jack said after I had finished catching him on current events.

"Explains what?"

"Well, some of my favorite people stopped by this morning asking about that book you're looking for. First the Fat Man and Little Boy came by, then the Triad came by an hour after that. They all wanted to know about the book, if I had heard of it, if anyone had hired us to find it, if I knew who might be selling it, that sort of thing. I played dumb, of course."

"I'm not surprised, you're good at that." I couldn't help myself. Fat Man is one of the big-league sorcerers around town, definitely in the Bookworm's league, possibly even more powerful. I never know exactly how to gauge these things. He's also enormously fat—hence the name—and has a reputation for stopping at nothing to get what he wants. Jack and I had done a job for the Fat Man years ago—I don't want to talk about the specifics—but it made us both feel kinda dirty, so we agreed not to take any more of his cases. He had gotten the message and hadn't been by the office since then. Little Boy is his apprentice. Way less powerful than Fat Man, and not quite as obese, but even creepier in some ways. That non-stop giggling of his has always bothered me. That and the fact that his breath smelled like something had crawled in his mouth and died.

"Asshole. Anyway, the Fat Man quickly realized that I didn't know anything about it—which I didn't until you just now told me about it—then they left. They were asking where you were and if you might know anything about it. Told 'em you were at home sleeping off a hangover with a trannie hooker you picked up last night. They had no problem believing that, so he and Little Boy decided to leave us alone."

"Thanks, Jack, you do wonders for my reputation around town." I actually found the whole thing a little troubling. The Fat Man is a pretty savvy guy, and I knew he was a ruthless S.O.B. I was hoping that I could quietly locate the book for the Bookworm without any interference and land an easy twenty grand. Guess life is never quite as easy as you hope it will be. My goal for the rest of the day was to studiously avoid bumping into the Fat Man.

"Look, kid, you know the source of the Fat Man's power, right?"

I shook my head no. I knew he was said to be pretty powerful, but I'd never heard how he got that way.

"He eats his enemies."

I could tell Jack was relishing this, stringing me along.

"What the fuck are you talking about?"

"You know, it's like how the Chinese eat tiger balls or dicks or whatever the fuck to become virile. Or cannibal tribes in New Guinea or Africa or wherever eat their enemies to gain their hunting skills or some such shit. Same thing with the Fat Man. He's found a way to make it really work. Same thing with his apprentice Little Boy, who ain't all that little. They eat their enemies, or parts of them at least, and somehow gain a measure of their power. Those two have got to be the baddest Pillsbury doughboys in town." I know when Jack is bullshitting me, and this wasn't one of those times. I was starting to feel a little queasy about the whole thing, but I forced myself to blow off my concerns about Fat Man and Little Boy. I wasn't going to drop the case just because a couple of fat freaks might be interested in the same book as me. Besides, it wasn't like I was standing between them and a gross of Twinkies. (No, something even better, the pessimistic part of my mind suggested.) Jack knew when to not push the issue and let it drop.

"So not more than an hour after our favorite fat men left, the Triad came in. All three of them."

"No. Fucking. Way."

"I've never actually seen them all in one place before. They were asking about the book too. By this point, even I was getting suspicious. They wanted to hire us to hunt down the book for them. I began to suspect that there was more to the story than they were letting on. I suspected that the Bookworm had already hired you to find the book, so I was noncommittal and told them we were pretty busy these days, and I'd call them back in a day or two if our schedules cleared up. I wanted to talk with you about the whole thing first."

The Triad is a group of, well, three sorcerers, oddly enough; two women and a man. They all look pretty much alike, dress alike, talk alike, act alike. From what we can tell, they're all linked somehow, and can freely swap each other's bodies, know what each other is thinking, that sort of thing. They work their magic together. I assume it's some kind of weird sex-based magic, but who the hell knows? They keep to themselves pretty much and don't get involved in much of the turf fighting that takes place in our local occult underground. They aren't supposed to be *that* nasty, but then again, you never really know what a wizard is up to. I didn't want to take any chances.

"Glad you declined gracefully, Jack. Very uncharacteristic of you. That would have been awkward as hell if two separate clients hired us to find the same book."

"Yeah, but as soon as you find the book, we could get the Bookworm and the Triad into a bidding war for it. . . ." Jack was gazing off into space and grinning evilly at the prospect of getting two wealthy clients to one up each other.

"No can do, Jack. You know I hate that kind of shit." Sometimes I'm too honorable for my own good, I guess. "I already told the Bookworm I'd find the book for him. If I find the book, it's his. No bidding wars or haggling, Jack."

"Besides," I added, "He's offering twenty grand for the book."

God, I love watching Jack snort coffee out of his nose.

He coughed, hacked, wheezed, and eventually set his favorite mug down—the one that hasn't been washed since I met him because he said the coffee residue adds to the flavor.

"Twenty grand?" he finally got out. "Jesus Christ! What's so special about the book? Why would anyone pay twenty grand for a lousy book?"

Jack's idea of a good book has lots of pictures in it. Preferably ones of bare breasts and freshly waxed pussy. I've loaned Jack a few books over the years, ones I thought he might like, but they were always returned worse for the wear and stinking of cigarettes, so I had long ago learned my lesson that Jack didn't really give a shit about books. That is, unless they were worth twenty grand to the right buyer. *That's* the kind of book Jack can get behind.

I started to tell Jack what the Bookworm had told me about the book when he stopped me, walked over to the door, jerked it open, looked outside and said, "I don't want to take any chances. It sounds like this has become pretty high stakes." He put out the closed sign, double-locked the door, and went over to his desk and started rummaging around. I've never figured out how he manages to find anything in that mess, but he always does, without fail. Every time I've tried to find something in Jack's half of the room, I've always come up empty-handed. Jack eventually pulled out some chalk, a couple candles, a dagger, you know, the usual magic ritual shit. I kicked back to enjoy the show. This was going to take a while. He sketched out a rough circle and some additional mystic symbols around it on our threadbare carpet, lit and placed the candles just so, traced some more symbols in the air with the point of the dagger, muttered a bunch of stuff I didn't catch and pronounced it safe to talk. Whatever. Jack's usual rigmarole. I had seen some crazy things since I first hooked up with Jack—and half of it was even real—but I could never make up my mind how much mystical shit Jack could actually do.

I went on to tell him everything I knew about the book and what Po Wen had told me about the Flea Market.

"Sounds like you're in this pretty deep, kid. I mean, on the face of it, it doesn't sound like that big of a deal, but given that the Fat Man and the Triad are both interested, well, that complicates matters a bit.

Be on your guard tonight at the Flea Market. I guess it all really depends on what you learn there. Hell, you might even stumble across the sap selling the book there. You could just buy it and drive right on over to the Bookworm. Case closed, and we're twenty grand richer for a day's work."

"Something tells me it's not going to be that easy, Jack."

"Yeah, I know, but I'm cautiously optimistic about this one. The ritual in the book sounds like it's scary as hell, so it's an important case, but it sounds like you're right on top of things."

I had my doubts, and he probably did as well, but we didn't lay those out on the table. Jack was always good about not damaging my self-confidence. We farted around and bullshitted about far more pleasant subjects than cannibal sorcerers and books sought after by heavy-hitting wizards for a couple of hours, then Jack told me about a case he was working on. The guy claimed that he had been stalked and harassed for the last two years. He was followed everywhere he went, received countless heavy breather phone calls, had pizzas and other food delivered every night he never ordered, had a bunch of magazine subscriptions and Franklin Mint collection items sent to him, and all that jazz. The guy claimed he had never knowingly made any enemies and had no idea who could be behind it. The sheer randomness of it all was really what was getting to him. Hard to say if it was true or not; for all we knew, the guy was a complete paranoid nutcase himself. Jack and I are happy to indulge paranoid nutjobs, of course, assuming they can pay our daily rate. This one could, and had pre-paid for a week of our time. Jack and I basically each work independently on different cases, but we brainstorm and help each other out as needed. I told Jack I'd start helping him with the paranoid's case as soon as I found the Bookworm's book. If everything went well, I should be working on a much more "normal" case in a day or two.

It was close to dinner time by this point, and Jack suggested we grab some Chinese carry-out at the place around the corner. I suspected he was as lonely for company as he was hungry. And maybe even just a touch nervous, given what I had told him about the book, as well as his stream of visitors during the day. Chinese was fine by me because my appetite for it had been whetted by the hot and sour soup I had earlier at Po Wen's. I know Chinese food runs the numbers up on Jack's diabetes, but hey, you only live once.

He doesn't give a shit, so why should I?

I always shuddered a little when I go to pick up food from the Chinese place, thinking of what the kitchen must look like. Can't think about it or you'd only eat stuff you grew yourself in a hermetically-sealed greenhouse. Besides, if my years of eating comped meals when I was working in the restaurant industry in my younger days didn't kill me, some crummy Chinese food tonight wouldn't either. Jack called in the order (he always gets the Kung Pao chicken, extra hot, and baby spareribs, and I ordered some of their excellent General Tso's chicken and some beef fried rice). I brought dinner back to the office for us, and Jack and I enjoyed our meals in companionable silence, then went back to talking about the usual: Jack scoring with the ladies, the latest "magical" trinket he had picked up, the Redskins, Howard Stern, etc. In a lot of ways, Jack was still a big immature kid, but in others he was the father and buddy rolled into one I had always wanted.

Jack volunteered to come with me to the Flea Market, but I knew he had already been planning to head to a hotel bar to pick up a desperate, aging businesswoman tonight, so I declined. Other than the magical trinkets, it was his only real hobby and I didn't want to intrude. Or have one of Jack's targets hit on me rather than him. That would have been *no bueno*.

Either I'd locate the book at the Flea Market, or at least a good solid lead on it, or I wouldn't. It shouldn't take both of us just to look around and talk with a couple people. Eventually I said my good-byes to Jack, he wished me happy hunting, and I took off.

It was about eight thirty by this point, so I drove down to Anacostia, getting warier and warier. Something about this whole set-up just didn't seem quite right, but I couldn't put my finger on it. I was probably just being a touch paranoid. The gang-bangers and drug dealers on every corner didn't exactly help ease my nerves. At least Lupo had a decent chain link fence with barb wire around his parking lot. I pulled up at the gate and rolled down my window. "I'm here for the Flea Market," I said eloquently to the gate attendant. He was a big guy, head completely shaved. He always wears a leather jacket zipped and buckled up tight, no matter what the weather is like. I had never learned his name, despite the fact that I had been coming to the Flea Market off and on for the last five years or so. He held out his hand, and I gave him the twenty that would gain me admission to the Flea Market. No acknowledgement or reply from Baldy, but he did at least open the gate for me. I drove through and sandwiched the Fiero between a minibus and an old-model Beetle.

The parking lot was full of cars but no people, so I headed inside. It was one big open room filled with tables and people milling around. Pretty much like any other flea market you'd find. The difference was most of these people were even weirder than the usual people who frequent flea markets—and that's saying something—and the types of junk being sold at the Flea Market weren't the usual *tchotchkes*, eight-tracks, and crocheted blankets. Some of the stuff here truly *was* magical. Real, honest-to-God magic. Most of it, however—like the stuff at any flea market—was just junk.

There was the same colorful assortment of freaks and weirdos tonight I had grown to expect. Of course the guy with the monkey was there. He's always there, just browsing. I gave them a wide berth; the monkey had thrown a little tiny poop pellet at me once. There was a man at a booth maintaining a constant chant of "Ghosts for sale! Ghosts in a bottle! Step right up and get your ghost in a bottle!" I idly wondered what someone would do with a ghost in a bottle, but didn't bother to ask him. Besides, he probably just blew some smoke in there and corked it real tight. Another guy sitting at a table across the way was selling his shadow. That's even less useful than a ghost in a bottle, unless I'm missing something. Besides, how desperate would you have to be to sell your own shadow? Passed him by too.

A homeless lady elbowed me out of her way in her haste to get at a long table heaped with crystals and trinkets and charms of all sorts. She maintained a constant mumble to herself as she pawed through the items (not that talking to yourself at the Flea Market is at all abnormal). I briefly considered picking up Jack a new little treat for his collection. Nah, best not to indulge the man his obsession.

I walked past the booth run by the First Church of Christ, Possessed. They scare the shit out of me. Their smiles are always just a little too fixed, and they're always dressed immaculately in their Sunday best, straight out of the fifties, with Windsor knots and plenty of Brylcreem. They have a booth at every Flea Market I've ever been to. Their wholesomeness is made even creepier by the fact that they are recruiting people to be possessed by demons, just like they are. I have to hand it to them, they are as fervent about converting people to their cause as any evangelical Christian I've ever met. I brushed aside the glossy pamphlet they thrust at me, being careful not to touch the hand holding the pamphlet. I forced myself not to shudder and kept moving. Not a single book in sight yet.

Some pretentious fuck calling himself "Duke Morpheo the Dream Merchant" had set up shop at the Flea Market as well. No thanks, I'm happy with my own private nightmares, don't need his as well. On second thought, I *had* been having those nightmares every night for a week. Couldn't hurt to talk with a self-professed "expert" about them, could it? I plopped down in a folding chair in front of his table. "So what's the deal here, buddy? How does this work?"

"Greetings and hallucinations, friend." Yes, that's what he actually said. He was a gawky little freak, skinny, but with a round little pot belly and a nasally voice. His hair was black and slicked back, but his temples were really starting to retreat. "Are you interested in purchasing a custom dream? You provide me with as much or as little information as you like, and I can guarantee you will have that dream the next time you sleep. I can also provide you with dream interpretation of past dreams you've experienced."

"Hang on just a second before we get into the whole spiel. What's your claim to fame? How did you become the 'Dream Merchant'?"

He seemed a little taken aback that I might question his credentials. "I started out as a simple oneiromancer...."

"A what?"

He sighed. But behind it, I knew he was still glad to give me the 411. "Well, a layman would probably describe it as a dream interpreter. But I have become so much more as my experience has grown. As I mentioned before, I have learned the art of inducing specific dreams in people. I can help free you from the drudgery of your daily existence. I can transport you to the dream world. I can help you experience your heart's desire any time you sleep."

I had him figured as a flake, but those nightmares have been starting to get to me. "OK, how about this: I tell you about this series of nightmares I've been having, and you tell me what the fuck it all means. How much for just that? No offense, but I'd rather not have you popping up in my dreams. I've got my own nightmares to worry about."

"Well, all right, if that's all you want. $20, cash up front."

I scowled a little, but handed it over to him. I proceeded to describe the nightmares: vague (and sometimes not so vague) feelings of dread, being consumed by something chasing me as I ran down the endless corridor lined with books, doom and gloom, ill omens, vultures feasting on my flesh, rats (rather than Jack Frost) nipping at my nose, being covered in flames but not being burned, rotting and corruption, etc., etc. All very cheery stuff, but I gave him everything I could remember.

He seemed to think about it a bit, then latched on to something I found interesting. "To me, the key is the endless corridor of books, while simultaneously being pursued by something you feel will consume you. You are clearly looking for something—a person, an item, a piece of information, perhaps a book even, though I don't want to interpret that part of your dreams too literally—while someone or something else is simultaneously seeking the same thing you seek. Whoever that is means to have the item at any cost and intends to kill anyone who gets in their way. I would advise you to use extreme caution in whatever this quest of yours is. I hesitate to say this, but your dreams don't bode well for you. Danger and suffering are very likely outcomes. Your subconscious understands this and is trying to warn your conscious mind to stay away from whatever this is through your repeated nightmares."

More good news. Well, that didn't tell me all that much, other than what I had already suspected. Still, it made a certain amount of sense. He might not be a complete flake...I'd have to think about this more when I had more time. The creepy thing for me, though, was that the nightmares began *before* I ever heard about the book. I still had a book to find. Nothing I could do about that now. I thanked him and headed on.

I waved to an old buddy of mine who calls himself the Watchmaker across the hall, despite the fact that he's a complete loon. He waved back, gave me a cross-eyed grin and shuffled off. That man is a whiz with machines. He can make any old piece of junk run like new, and he can cobble together pretty much anything you'd ever need out of random spare parts—robots, death-rays, a new carburetor, you name it. Senile as hell, but you can't win them all. I'd had him help me in the past with my Fiero. Extremely cheap, and more skilled than any professional mechanic I'd ever used before.

Someone tapped me on the shoulder. Shit, it was the Snow Witch. She gave me her best enigmatic smile, exhaling a hint of frost as she said, "Hello, Augustino."

I rubbed my shoulder trying to massage some of the cold out of it where she had touched me. "How's it going there, Frosty Lady?" I turned on the charm, despite the fact that my arms were now covered in goosebumps, and my balls had just retracted into my body as far as they would go. She tends to have that effect on me.

I've been seeing the Snow Witch around town for the last few years. I swear to God, the last three winters have been some of the coldest in DC I remember. Coincidence?

She's a good looking woman, probably mid-to-late thirties, though she still had perfect complexion and milky white skin. Not a wrinkle on her. The sun had probably never even touched her. Hair so black and shiny, it almost certainly had to be dyed. She always wore white. Tonight was no different; she was wearing a white pleather pantsuit that hugged every curve of her body, I couldn't help but notice. "Oh I'm doing fine. Haven't seen you around lately. You haven't been hiding from me, have you?"

"Who, me? Why would I hide from a lovely lady like you? I'm just playing hard to get, that's all."

She arched one eyebrow. "Well then, in that case, why don't we have dinner together one night soon. You can come over to my place, and I'll make a nice meal of . . . I mean, *for* you." I couldn't quite tell if that was a joke or a warning. Could be either. Or both.

She wasn't normally this aggressive. Not that we were more than occasional acquaintances. It surprised me a little. Usually *I'm* the hunter. "Let me guess, we'd have cold cuts, with ice cream for dessert?" I was pretty sure she could take a joke like that, and it gave me time to think.

She obliged me with a quick laugh. Her laugh was a little more girlish than I had imagined. She was waiting for my reply.

"Sure, I'd love to. Why don't you give me your number and—"

"Uh-uh. I know how that little game works. Give me *your* number, Augustino, and I'll call you. Soon."

I made a big show of sighing and feigning hurt that she didn't trust me, but I gave her my number. Oddly, I found myself looking forward to that dinner more than I had expected. Not that I needed any more distractions in my life right now.

"Well, I need to get going, I'm on the clock." She waved, walked off, turned around and blew me a kiss. It just about froze my cheek off where it landed.

I didn't know whether I should be happy or scared about our upcoming dinner date.

I glanced over to the side, behind a row of tables and spotted a couple of the Munchkins prowling around in one corner of the warehouse. Ugly little fuckers. They're a pack of midgets who live underground and mostly keep to themselves, except when they get hungry or see someone pretty. They don't like pretty. They *really* don't like pretty. Were they after the Snow Witch? Not sure why I felt protective, that lady could certainly protect herself from a couple of ugly dwarves. Nope, they weren't paying her any particular attention, just generally lurking around. Charming. No way I was getting any closer to them than I absolutely had to, definitely no need to get tangled up with them. I watched them slink off into the shadows in the back of the warehouse, and I didn't see them again.

I had to keep moving, making sure I covered the entire Flea Market. The book had to be here somewhere. I was scanning across the books spread out on someone's table, but they were all New Age crap, mostly paperbacks. Nothing old and leatherbound as far as the eye could see (unless you count the old ladies selling stuff). I felt a hand grab my shoulder and whip me around.

Oh, shit. He had all the hallmarks of the Bloodchildren: black clothes, spiky hair, big boots, bad attitude, teeth filed down to points.

"Hey, asshole!" he snarled. "We haven't forgotten about you."

Some nearby do-gooder saw what was going on and said "Hey, you know the Flea Market is neutral territory! No fights, no grudges here." Like that would stop a feral Bloodchild from trying to rip me to shreds or suck all my precious bodily fluids dry.

"Shut the fuck up and mind your own business!" he nimbly retorted without even sparing a glance for the Good Samaritan.

He grabbed the front of my shirt and said, "I know you're the one who grabbed our girl. I hope you're happy. You cost her a chance at eternal life. We don't like it when people poke their noses into our business. You'd better watch your back—I'll be back in a minute with some friends of mine who would love to see you again." I didn't like that pointy-toothed smile one bit.

I gave him a good shove. He strutted away, giving me the finger as he went.

OK, better get a move on and find this book fast.

The problem was, by this point, I had made all the rounds. The book wasn't anywhere obviously for sale at the Flea Market. Nobody even came close to looking like the buyer or seller of a book like the one I was looking for. I had checked with the couple of booksellers here tonight, and nothing had rung a bell. Po Wen's information was very rarely wrong. So where was the damn book? Just one person left to ask.

I spotted Lupo, the Flea Market Grand Poobah, being hectored by some old lady selling crystals and geodes. Lupo was wearing his typical uniform, a nasty-ass wife beater with yellow stains under the pits and old chinos. His comb-over was looking even more sparse than usual tonight. Plenty of matted black fur peeking out of his wifebeater though. Hair from his head must have migrated south for the winter. Since I wasn't having any luck myself, I figured if anyone knew of a valuable book being brought to the Flea Market, Lupo would.

I told him roughly what I was looking for, and asked him where I might be able to find it, since none of the usual booth sellers had anything even loosely fitting the bill.

Lupo was looking even more shifty than usual. "Oh man, I'm sorry, Augustino, you're too late. I think someone did bring the book that you're looking for in earlier, but it was sold at a private, invitation-only auction before tonight's Flea Market began."

"You sold it at a private, *invitation-only* auction before the Flea Market even began? Since when do you do that? What the fuck is going on here, Lupo?" I was upset, to say the least. Shocked begins to start to cover it. "Are you getting delusions of grandeur in your old age? Look at this place, it's not Sotheby's of London! And you're not exactly some high-roller auctioneer. What do you know about running an auction?"

"Come on, Augustino, that's not fair! This was a one-of-a-kind deal. The seller requested that I invite a select few clientele he specifically named earlier this afternoon, and that's what I did. Got 15% of the selling price too, just like a real auction house! It was a pretty sweet deal for me, hell, for everybody. For whatever reason, the seller didn't invite you or whoever you're working for. Nothing I can do about that," Lupo said with an insincere shrug. "I only invited the people he named. I wasn't going to bring in anybody else he didn't want and queer the deal."

"So who was this mysterious seller?"

"I don't know who the guy was, dude. You don't know him either. Just some guy named Roger. From Philly, I think he said."

"Some 'dude' named Roger, huh? Are you shitting me, Lupo? Just some guy from out of town who wanted to set up this auction out of the blue?"

"Would I lie to you, Augustino?"

I didn't bother to answer that. "So he just came in, took his money, and left. Lemme guess, you have no idea where he is now?"

"Nope, I sure don't. He's gone. Damn, I hope he's doing all right. Roger didn't look so hot, come to think of it. All pasty and sweating and shit. Had a big-ass bandage wrapped around his hand. Man, you don't think he had something, like, catching, do you? " Lupo felt his forehead, then pressed on his lymph nodes. "I do *not* need to be getting sick. Got a hot date tomorrow night. Real easy bitch too, if you know what I mean. Just give her a little meth and—"

I cut him off. "Nah, Lupo, you look fit as a fiddle, I wouldn't worry about it. You're gonna be just fine for your lady friend. If I catch up with Roger, I'll pass along your concern about his health though."

I thought about it a second. "OK, OK, if you really already helped sell the book, then I guess it's out of my hands. But you can at least tell me who bought it."

"Sorry, Augustino, no can do. The seller swore me to absolute secrecy on the whole thing. I've only told you this much because you're such a swell guy." God, I love such heartfelt enthusiasm.

"OK, Lupo, this is a serious deal here, I'm not kidding around. I really need to know who the buyer of the book was."

"Aw, come on, Augustino, you can't honestly expect me to tell you who the buyer was. I'm a businessman, I have to maintain my clients' anonymity . . . ."

"Fifty bucks." He shook his head no and crossed his arms. I sighed and said "A hundred bucks if you give me the name of the buyer right now."

"Money up front."

I peeled off five twenties and thrust them into his grubby paws.

"It was that weird guy who works for the Lich. You know the one, never says much? Maybe he's mute or something? Just hands you a note when he needs to say something."

Yeah, I knew him. The Lich never leaves his home. Lupo was talking about the Lich's errand boy and lackey. I'd never heard what the guy's name was. There was something not quite right about him, but I could never put my finger on it exactly.

I didn't bother asking Lupo to keep my knowledge of the buyer secret from the next person who came along and asked, since that would have been futile and a waste of money (obviously). Fat chance I could get the book away from the Lich, but a guy had to try, didn't he? Besides, I was playing with the Bookworm's money at this point, and he had a lot to throw around.

I headed out to my car for the Lich's house in Foxhall before the friendly neighborhood Bloodchild I had met inside could return with friends. As I was walking up to the car, I noticed someone standing next to it. One of the women of the Triad. Damn, this was not turning out to be my night. "Hello, Augustino," she said in a monotone voice. Plain-looking, long shaggy hair starting to turn grey, nondescript clothes, and hooded eyes that didn't quite focus on me. "Your partner probably told you that we stopped by. We were interested in hiring you two to procure an item for us, but your partner did not seem interested in the job."

"Oh, hey. You know how it goes, business is booming. We just can't take all the cases that come our way these days, have to turn down some prospective customers, unfortunately. Maybe next time?" Sometimes I'm a shitty liar (like now), but she didn't react.

"We came here tonight looking for the item we seek, but it did not turn up."

"We?" I looked around for the others, but didn't see anyone.

"Yes, we did not have any luck. Have you heard anything about the item? We think you know what we mean."

"Nope, I'm not entirely sure I do know what you mean. Jack didn't tell me much, but I haven't heard any rumblings around town about any new special books. Tell you what though: if I do hear anything, you'll be the first person, er, people I call."

She didn't reply, and I brushed past her, being careful not to actually touch her—I have this thing about not getting mojo'ed without my permission—and got in the car. I shivered involuntarily, whether it was due to the night air or something else, I'm not sure. She wasn't anywhere to be seen by the time I looked in the rear view mirror. I rolled out of there as fast as I could.

Some people just give me the creeps.

INTERLUDE

Roger had the money in hand from the auction. The book was finally out of his hands and in the hands of...whoever that guy who bought it was. It was more money than Roger had ever seen in one place in his life. So why wasn't he happy? His head was throbbing—worse than ever—and he couldn't stop sweating. He was wracked with chills every few minutes. Maybe it was the flu? He didn't even want to think about his hand and those crazy old Masonic fucks.

And now he couldn't even rest for a minute and think in his own goddamn car because his girlfriend didn't know when to shut the hell up.

"Roger, this is insane! This whole thing is completely crazy, you've been acting even weirder than normal. I'm worried. We've got to get you to a doctor. We should—"

Mary had a car key sticking out of the side of her neck. The bitch had finally stopped talking. Roger pulled the key out. Blood poured out, covering his hand in hot stickiness. She was still trying to talk, the crazy bitch. She would never shut up. He stuck the key back in the hole, rooted around in there a bit. Rooted around in there like a little mouse, looking for a snack, nibbling at cheese.... Roger giggled.

He carefully buckled Mary in—"Don't want you getting hurt, do we, baby?" Roger went to start the car off and remembered that the key was, well, he wiped it off on his pants. He stuck the key in the ignition and it started up, smooth as silk. Thank God the key hadn't bent. He drove slowly and carefully through the city, ending up in Southwest DC down by the waterfront overlooking Hains Point. He put the car in neutral and stared out into the black Potomac. No one around. DC at night in the winter can be a very dark place indeed.

Roger wasn't there anymore. There was really nothing of him left in the bag of flesh that rolled down the windows, revved the engine, put the car in drive, and gunned it over the embankment, catching some air and sinking into the Potomac.

CHAPTER 6

The Lich had arrived in DC a few years ago, and Jack and I have done the occasional job for him. He's one of our stranger clients, but he's knowledgeable and doesn't mind throwing his money around to get what he wants, so he's on Jack's and my list of "good guys." I think he's from somewhere in Europe, though I'm not sure—he has a faint accent of some kind, but I can't place it. Hell, he could just be from Minnesota, I have no idea. He's only available at night, and he never leaves his house. He does pay us to come by for house calls though. He's an odd one, that's for sure.

The Lich lives in the far corner of Northwest DC in a very ritzy, very private neighborhood. Lots of old, old money and privacy fences. Just the way he likes it, I assume. Rich people always value discretion. I drove up Foxhall, then started taking some back streets. It sure was dark back there. Good thing I knew where I was going. Guess the rich don't want the riffraff to be able to find their houses in the dark.

I eventually arrived at the Lich's place, parked on the street, walked through his gate, and rang the bell. Rang it again after there was no answer. Come on, man, open the damn door. I knew he was home, he never leaves his house. Rang it some more for good measure.

Finally, someone opened the door a crack, didn't say anything. I knew it wasn't the Lich because he doesn't answer his own door. "My name is Augustino. I'm here to see the Lich. He knows me." The door shut silently. I waited longer. Finally, the door opened again. A tall man with thinning hair and dead eyes stepped out of my way so I could enter. He was wearing a shabby, threadbare suit, and I could have sworn that his face had dust in the creases. He started walking away from me, so I assumed he wanted me to follow him down the darkened hallway. There didn't appear to be any lights on in the house, and the drapes weren't letting much light in. Very inviting. He walked into the parlor and briefly pointed at a chair, then shuffled off, back the way we came.

"Hey can we turn some lights on in this place?" I asked, but Lurch had already walked away and didn't acknowledge me. I found the light switch and flicked it. One lousy lamp on an end table came on. Great, a forty watt bulb to light up an entire house. The place was covered in a fine film of dust. It looked like someone's spinster aunt had decorated the place. I plopped down in a plastic covered armchair and figured I'd be waiting some more.

I must have just shut my eyes for a second, because when I opened them and looked up, the Lich was standing in front of me. He was wearing a blue silk dressing gown. His skin was papery and paler than any I had ever seen. His eyes are ice blue and bulgy, and the top of his head is covered by thin little wisps of white hair. I knew better than to try to shake his hand. The Lich doesn't like to be touched—I found that out the hard way the first time I met him; Jack, being the nice guy that he is, thought it would be funny not to mention that—but I can guarantee that shaking hands with him is an experience I wouldn't want to repeat. And, judging by his scandalized squawking at the time, neither would he.

"Hello, Augustino." His voice was quiet, and I had to strain to hear him. "What brings you to my home today? You come unbidden." Yes, the Lich is the kind of guy who uses words like "unbidden." You could say he's truly "old school." Like, from the seventeenth century or so.

"Well, I'm sorry to bother you, Lich, I'm sure you're a busy guy, but I was interested in locating something I thought might have recently come into your possession." No reaction, but then again, the Lich never reacts, so I just blathered on.

"I'm looking for a book. I think you know the one I'm talking about. *The Thirty-third Esoteric Key of the Invisible Lodge.* I believe that you purchased it earlier today. My client is interested in purchasing the book from you and will entertain any reasonable amount you might put on the book."

Long pause. "Who is your client?"

That would be telling. "I should say that if you are concerned that my client is a rival sorcerer who might use the ritual described in the book against you, please don't be. While I can't reveal who my client is, I can assure you that he intends to destroy the book so that no one can use the ritual it describes. I'm sure it can be arranged that the book could be destroyed in your presence, or you could receive other reasonable assurances. We can discuss those arrangements if you're willing to sell the book to me and my client. What do you say? You could make a tidy profit on reselling the book, and I can guarantee you that the information the book contains will never be used against you or any of your interests."

He replied in slow motion, like he always does. "Your client's concern about the uses to which I might put the book is commendable; however, I assure you that the book is in my safekeeping and will not be used for the purpose you fear. I acquired the book for my own reasons. Because you seem concerned, and because you have been a trusted associate in the past, I will tell you that I do not intend to perform the ritual described in the book. Neither will I destroy the book nor otherwise enable its destruction, however. I have sought the book for my own purposes, on which I will not further elaborate."

"Look, Lich, I'm not trying to be a dick here, but I really need to see the book. I'm concerned because there are some extremely ruthless people after this book, people who will stop at nothing to get it. That includes the Fat Man and the Triad. You know they're all pretty serious dudes. And dudettes, for that matter. Anyway, for my own peace of mind, I need to know that the book is safe in your hands. It's my understanding that something might have happened to the book after it came into your possession." I was basically bluffing. I had no reason to believe that anything bad had happened to the book once the Lich bought it, or that the Fat Man knew where the book was. It seemed pretty clear to me that the Triad didn't have a clue where the book was. Otherwise, why harass me in the parking lot of the Flea Market? I really just felt like I had to keep him talking and try to at least see the book, rather than have him just show me the door. I knew I was close to it and I didn't want to have to tell the Bookworm I sucked and couldn't get the book for him. If that meant throwing around the Fat Man's or the Triad's names to scare some sense into the Lich, then so be it.

The Lich pondered for a long, long time. "Very well, if you insist, I will check on the book. I only just received it a few hours ago. I assure you, it is safe. My sanctum is heavily warded, and I would know immediately if anyone had tampered with the book or any of my other possessions. I will show you the book so that you are satisfied it is in my safekeeping, but you may not read it or borrow it. The book remains with me. That is not negotiable." I exhaled a big sigh of relief. At least I'd get a chance to take a look at it, make sure it was the book I was after, and see what all the fuss was about. And see where he kept it and maybe even get an idea of what kind of security he had on it; that might be worth some bucks to the Bookworm even if I couldn't acquire it myself. I hated the idea of having to return to the Bookworm and tell him that there was no way I could retrieve the book, but at least I could tell him who currently had the book. That all had to be worth *something* to him, even if it meant kissing the full twenty grand away.

The Lich led me into another, mostly empty room and opened the door to what I would have thought was a closet or pantry. There were steps leading down. The Lich led me slowly down the steps into his basement. I found myself strangely anxious and wanting to bolt around him to check on the book. It was like being stuck behind a tourist on a Metro escalator watching my train roll in and not being able to get to the platform. Fortunately, I was able to contain myself. I'm good like that. Besides, bolting down a set of unfamiliar stairs into a pitch black basement in the home of a sorcerer who might or might not be fully living is not my idea of a good time. I asked him if there was a light we could turn on. He didn't reply, but reached up with one of his long arms and pulled on a chain from the ceiling. A flickering forty watt bulb illuminated a ten foot radius. Better than nothing, I guess. At least the Lich's monthly electric bill every month was pretty low.

We walked to a small door covered in chains and glyphs. "Please wait here. I will check on the book, and bring it out to you so that you may see it is safe." He pressed his hands against the door, and it opened soundlessly. Darkness within, so I couldn't see what was in there.

Dead silence, then I heard a strangled sound, and I ran into the vault. The Lich was just standing there. In the dim light I could see that his mouth was hanging open, with no sound coming out. His eyes were bugged almost out of his skull. Not a pleasant sight.

Inside the vault was a small bricked-in chamber. Pretty bare bones, except for a small wooden table and an old reading stand or podium. Part of the back wall was caved in, with bricks spilling onto the floor. The caved in area was about three feet tall and two or three feet wide. I couldn't see very far back in there because of the Lich's unwholesome fascination with keeping his house as dark as possible, but from what I could see, the tunnel went back a ways. No book in sight anywhere.

Statement of the obvious time: "I assume that tunnel isn't supposed to be there?"

He shook his head slightly, mouth still open. I could have counted all his teeth if I had wanted.

"So someone tunneled into your basement and stole the book? Jesus Christ! What the hell is going on here?"

He seemed to recover from his shock a little. "Don't say that name here."

I looked askance at him. Some of these wizard types take the act a little too far for my liking. "OK, but seriously, who could have tunneled into your basement without you knowing about it and just to take the book? You said the whole place was warded, right? Magical protections and all that jazz? How could those be penetrated without you knowing it?"

His reply came lightning fast—for him—only taking five or six seconds. "It would have had to be done by someone knowledgeable in magic. I admit, though, that I did not anticipate the brick wall crumbling and weakening the runes. I could hardly foresee that someone would silently burrow through living earth to enter my basement. I will, of course, rectify that gap in my sanctum's defenses momentarily."

I pretty much ruled out Fat Man and his apprentice Little Boy. No way those two fatties could have even fit inside that tunnel, much less crawled down it, snatched the book, and crawled back out. The members of the Triad could probably have squeezed in through the tunnel, but it just didn't feel like it would be the Triad's style at all. Those three just didn't strike me as the tunnel rat types. Besides, unless the brief encounter in the parking lot was a complete ruse, they didn't seem to know who had the book. I knew that only someone or someones who were small enough to fit in the tunnel, and who had a strong connection to the DC underground—else why choose that route?—could have tunneled into the Lich's basement. Who else would have gone the underground route? Not many people I knew were more interested in what was *under* DC than what was happening in the buildings and byways of the city.

The only group I could think of that was small enough and had the underground connection thing going was the Munchkins. And, come to think of it, I had seen a couple of those little fuckers prowling around at the Flea Market. Could they have been there trying to get a hold of the book too? Not a bad guess. Certainly a possibility to consider. It was worth checking out. Right then, it was my only lead, but Jesus, I wasn't relishing the prospect of seeking them out in their tunnels.

The Lich called after me faintly as I dashed upstairs, "Remember, Augustino, the book is mine. If you recover it, I'll pay you handsomely for its return." Yeah, you and every other freak in town. I brushed past Lurch and ran out to my car. I knew where the Munchkins lived, but getting the book back from them—assuming they even had it—was *not* going to be easy.

CHAPTER 7

I had a strong inkling I knew where the Munchkins could be found this time of night: everyone said they lived in the abandoned streetcar tunnels under Dupont Circle. The underground streetcar tunnels were built back in the '40s, but were closed up a couple decades later when DC did away with its streetcars. They tried to renovate part of the tunnels in the late '90s and turn them into a commercial area called "Dupont Down Under." A very bad, very cheesy idea, it quickly went bust, but not before the city tarted the area up a bit down there. I had heard rumblings that the Munchkins moved in a few years ago after the city abandoned it (again) and made it their own. I didn't know of anyone who had been down there in years—the Munchkins didn't exactly encourage visitors, and no one I had ever met had made a habit of bothering them.

As I said, the Munchkins had a pretty nasty reputation. There were so many bizarre rumors and tales swirling around our little local occult scene about them that it was even harder than usual to separate fact from fiction. The freak community thrives on rumors, innuendo, and outright lies, so I never knew quite what to believe. All I knew is that they were said to be just about the nastiest, most vicious suckers in the area. Some said they were cannibals. Others said they were sex fiends. (That part is probably true, but then again who isn't a sex fiend or a cannibal in DC?) They were "known" to kidnap people and do things to them, but it was never clear exactly what. Hell, for all I knew, they were friendly little fellows who were just misunderstood. Wouldn't be the first time that an urban legend had proved to be false.

Yeah, right.

I drove around and around the various side streets of Dupont looking for a spot I could wedge my car into. The only people out at this time of night in mid-winter were drunks, college students, gays cruising for a good-night kiss, and the ever-present DC meter maids. I already had so many unpaid parking tickets, I was pretty sure they would call for a tire boot the next time I got one. Sure, I could always cut it off with Jack's acetylene torch, but God, what a pain. I finally found a spot after driving around for way too long. I made a mental note to stay the hell away from Dupont Circle for a while. The main entrances to the tunnels were locked up tight as a drum, but I knew you could still access them through a couple manholes and steam vents on the side streets. Some buddies and I had spent a whole summer exploring the tunnels under DC back in high school. Let's hope my memory was serving me correctly, and the city hadn't blocked anything off. I had zero interest in wandering around lost in the dark or getting blasted by live steam or electricity. I grabbed my Maglite from the trunk and headed out.

I found a loose steam vent cover and pried it up, then lowered myself down, replacing the cover loosely so I could push it aside in a hurry if I needed to. There were a couple homeless guys and a semi-drunk college kid looking for pot and/or a blowjob who might have seen me head down into the tunnel, but I couldn't worry about that now. I'd just have to take my chances. Besides, it's not like the DC cops were going to organize a tunnel raid based on the word of a couple drunk guys who claimed they saw a guy go down there.

I really, really, *really* didn't want to do this. Don't get me wrong, I've done plenty of stupid, foolhardy, maybe even the occasional brave things in my life, but this had to be one of the dumbest I've ever thought about doing. For God's sake, I was about to go crawling around in underground tunnels to retrieve a book stolen by a pack of sinister cannibal sex fiend midgets! Hell, the little bastards might not have even been the ones who took the book. That would be an ironic end for me—killed and raped and eaten (order not yet determined) by midgets I had wrongly accused of stealing some stupid book they didn't know anything about.

At least it was considerably warmer down here in the tunnels than up on the street. It was almost uncomfortably warm down here. But holy shit, were there a lot of rats down in the tunnels! These were even bigger than the alley rats you see when you're heading back to your car after a late night of drinking. They weren't even afraid of me. Hell, they didn't even bother to scurry out of my way. I crushed one's back beneath my shoe accidentally. Fucker wouldn't move out of my way. Served him right. I think the others starting keeping their distance a little more after I crushed their buddy. It was still more than a little eerie every time my flashlight caught a pair of eyes in its beam. The floors were covered in mud and other unnamed filth. There wasn't much actual standing water, but the whole place was damp, and there was just enough muck to make your feet stick to the ground slightly and splatter your pants with crap. The ceilings were actually pretty tall (they had to accommodate trolley cars, after all), and the tunnels were wide enough for half a dozen people or more to walk abreast. I found myself passing several smaller side tunnels—for maintenance, I assumed—and closed and locked doors. I decided to stick with the main tunnel for now. I didn't want to get lost down here, and I thought the likeliest place to find the colony of Munchkins would be the main tunnel.

I wended my way down the tunnel for a ways, then my flashlight caught a couple pairs of eyes. Big eyes. Eyes positioned about four feet off the floor. Couldn't be rats that big, just floating in the middle of the tunnel. The eyes moved forward a bit.

"Hello?"

Nothing.

Well, I knew they had spotted me at this point. That was what I came here for, I guess. I called out "I'm here to see the Munchkins." God, how I wanted to say "The Wizard" instead of "Munchkins." Figured they probably wouldn't find Oz jokes that all that funny. "Take me to your leader."

Dead silence.

Whispers and movement.

My flashlight was starting to flicker.

Fuck. This was not the time for the batteries to go. I swore to God I'd change the batteries every week if these would just last me another few minutes.

I sensed more than saw movement both in front of and behind me.

Yep, I had definitely found the Munchkins, all right, or at least they had found me.

#

They led me back, deeper into the tunnels, and went into a side tunnel to where I assumed they lived. They kept urging me forward, pushing me, occasionally digging into my arms or back with their sharp little fingernails. I really didn't need a bunch of little crescent-shaped cuts with God knows what in them. I didn't want to go too fast, I had no idea where they were taking me, and my Maglite was still flickering a bit. I was thinking of suing the battery company if I ever made it out of here alive. I saw that they were pushing me toward another Munchkin standing in the middle of the tunnel with his arms crossed. He was a disgusting little freak who I took to be their leader. He was naked and covered in muck, with wild greasy hair and a long beard. (Yes, his penis was preternaturally large, why do you ask, you sick fuck? I did my best not to look at it.) His eyes were huge and strikingly blue as they looked up at me and slowly blinked. "I am Gristle," he said in a surprisingly deep voice. "What do you want with us?"

The way out of here, I thought, looking around at the pack of Munchkins clustered around us. Jesus, there were fifteen or twenty of the little critters. Half a dozen were touching me with their filthy little fingers. "My name is Augustino. Maybe you've heard of me?" He didn't reply. "Yeah, probably not. That's cool. Anyway, um, I'm interested in something you and your associates might have acquired earlier today. A book."

"What kind of book? What makes you think we have this book?"

I caught a quick movement out of the corner of one eye. I could have sworn I saw one of Po Wen's little homunculi watching us with its beady little rat eyes from a perch in the shadows, but when I looked more closely, I couldn't be sure. Could have been a rat. Could have been anything, or nothing at all, my imagination was wound pretty tight right about now. Well, if it was one of Po Wen's little friends, he'd know about the progress of my investigation soon enough.

"Well, I know that the book was taken in a very clever fashion from the Lich's home. I know that you are probably the only ones in the entire city who could have taken it from him, especially by breaking into his basement through a tunnel, and given the skill involved. And I know that you all are likely the only ones who could have known that the Lich had just taken possession of the book. There aren't many people in the city who could have pulled that one off, so I came looking for you." I figured a little flattery couldn't hurt. Gristle and his cronies seemed to accept my words at face value. They hadn't added me to the stewpot yet, anyway.

"If we did have this book, why would we give it to you? What would you do with it? If we do have the book, we would have gone to considerable trouble to get it. We would not want the Lich to get his hands on the book and use it against us because he believes that we took it from him. We know the book is valuable, highly sought after . . ." Gristle's smile showed every one of his sharp little teeth.

"Look, Gristle, I just want the book for my own purposes. I'm not working for the Lich, and I'm not going to simply give it back to him. I can assure you that I will personally make sure that the Lich never gets his hands on the book, as a matter of fact. The Lich need never know that I retrieved the book from you. I certainly won't tell him if you won't." Gristle was a hard one to read, and I couldn't tell if he was convinced or not.

Then I noticed a naked girl—not a Munchkin, a normal sized girl—squatting in the corner. She had shoulder length, dirty blonde hair and was sitting hunched over so I couldn't see her face. She looked up briefly, then back down quickly. I could see why—she was hideous. Her face was all twisted, almost a little melted looking. Maybe a burn victim? No, her skin tone was uniformly colored—dirt.

Wait a second. She looked over at me again, into my eyes briefly. I recognize that girl. Or at least, I recognize what she *used* to look like. What was left of her face was still unmistakable. She was this gorgeous stripper who used to work at Camelot downtown. Best strip club in the city. Er, I've heard. Anyway, I'd remember her anywhere. Gorgeous, incredibly sexy, giant fake tits to die for, blonde hair, and most memorably, she was over six feet tall. She was close to 6'6" in those stripper shoes with the clear heels. I go to a strip joint maybe a couple times a year, and Camelot was my strip club of choice. Used to date a chick who worked there, years ago, so I always had a soft spot for the place, and the girls there didn't give you the hard sell if you're a cheap bastard like me. No way I'd ever forget this chick. For the life of me I couldn't remember her stage name, but it had to be her. She had been unbelievably hot and fairly down-to-earth, for a stripper at least. She was out to take guys' money away from them, but at least she had always been nice about it.

"Do you like what we've done with her?" Gristle leered when he saw me looking at her. "She was so pretty when we got her. So very pretty and tall. Now she's…not so pretty to look at. Or nearly as tall. But she's so fun to play with…." He broke off in peels of high-pitched laughter. His cohorts chortled and snorted.

I forced myself not to shudder, and I looked away from her.

Gotta focus on the matter at hand, Augustino. First the book, then we'll see what we can do about the girl. "So how much do you want for the book?"

Bargaining with Gristle and the Munchkins was excruciatingly painful, kind of like trying to buy a used car from the biggest con artist in the world. Two things eventually became clear though. One, they clearly had the book, but I'd bet dollars to doughnuts that they hadn't understood a word that was written in the book. That had to be why they were willing to part with the book even though they had obviously gone to so much trouble to get their paws on it. While they were clearly clued in on some level with magic—witness the plight of the stripper huddled in the corner and the fact that they made it into and out of the Lich's basement alive and without him knowing about it—they had no idea what to do with the book once they got it. And more importantly, they knew it was beyond them and they'd never be able to figure it out. And two, what Gristle eventually got around to telling me, was that what the Munchkins *really* wanted was food.

The Munchkins' idea of a gourmet feast apparently consisted of Spam. Tin after tin of Spam, with that gooey clear gelatin ladled on top for dessert.

I knew I was going to regret this, but I had to ask: "Why Spam?"

Gristle just smiled.

"No, really. You guys are willing to trade the book for a large enough quantity of *Spam*? Why do you guys like Spam so much?" Sometimes I can be very naïve.

Gristle's smile got wider. "It tastes like people."

That was a good enough explanation for me, I didn't want to hear any more about it. We finally settled on half a truckload of Spam. I was pretty sure the Bookworm would cover this as a "reasonable" expense in order to acquire the book, so I wasn't *too* worried. Hell, for all I knew, a half of truckload of Spam might cost more than the twenty grand the Bookworm was paying me as my commission, so I certainly wasn't going to cover it out of my share. But damn, this was going to be the oddest looking expense report I had ever turned in to a client.

"So why did you guys want the book originally anyway?" I couldn't help but ask after we were finished dickering.

Gristle gave me a long, appraising look. "Its scent," he finally said quietly. "Its scent . . . we could smell it as soon as it came into the city. The cover . . ." he shuddered here a bit. "The cover smelled . . . delicious . . . ."

Right. The cover was human leather and probably permeated by magic. Of course it smelled delicious to these freaks.

"But once we got our hands on the book, and looked through it," he continued, as though their attraction to a human leather-covered book was the most natural thing in the world, "we realized how foul and disgusting it is—we don't want it anymore."

I didn't know what to say to that, so I decided to return to the unresolved issue of the terrified stripper in the corner. "The girl looks like she's pretty much all used up, but I think I could still have a little fun with her. Why don't you throw her in with the book to sweeten the deal?" God, I felt dirty, but it was for her own good.

Gristle considered this for a while, though he looked at me like he thought I was crazy. "The girl won't last much longer. We're almost done with her. She won't be of much use to you." Gristle shrugged. "You can have her for a litter of kittens . . . ."

I balked at that just a twinge, I really did, even though it was a girl's life on the line.

"I'm guessing you and your friends would like to have a side order of kittens along with your Spam?"

He looked at me like I was a child molester who had just proposed raping a baby in front of him. "No! We just want to train some nice, pretty little kitties to hunt rats for us."

Weird, but I could live with it. They'd better be some pretty tough kittens though, some of the rats I saw while coming in could bench press more than I can.

I agreed, and Gristle made a gesture. A couple of the Munchkins went over to the girl, slapped her face a bit and made her stand. She was kind of bent over, and I still couldn't get a good look at her body. It definitely didn't look the same as when she was on stage at Camelot. They pinched and prodded her until she made it over to me, then they pushed her in my direction. I caught her, and she whimpered. "It's going to be all right, I won't hurt you. I'll get you out of here, and you'll be safe," I whispered to her so the Munchkins couldn't hear me. She was sobbing uncontrollably. Jesus, what had they been doing to her down here?

Gristle wanted me to shake his hand to seal the deal. I have to say, I can't remember when I've ever done something so distasteful. Oh well, I could always pour bleach all over it or cut it off when I got home.

Gristle had two of his henchdwarves bring me the book. They carried it carefully between them. It was sealed in a scuffed-up leather case. I wiped my hands on my jeans to get off the larger bits of filth, then carefully lifted it out of the case, not wanting to get any of the filth that covered me onto the book. Yep, the cover and binding looked just as the Bookworm had described. I eventually got the book opened to the title page. That checked out too. So this was the book that everyone wanted so badly. I flipped through it. Frankly, it didn't look that impressive. Sure, it was kind of cool that it was one of Ben Franklin's books, but it didn't look amazing enough to be worth twenty grand. I wondered if the Bookworm was just being paranoid about the book containing a ritual that could be used to contact Tiamat. Hell, for all I knew, Tiamat was a purely mythological being and Ben Franklin sampled a little too much corn whiskey while he was writing his book.

"Remember, Augustino, you will hold up your end of the bargain, or we will ensure that you live to regret it. Our kind is not to be trifled with!"

"Not to worry, Gristle, ol' buddy. I'm a man of my word. You'll have your Spam, and your kittens too. Within a week, I swear. It's going to take a little time to get that much Spam together. You know how it goes. Say, can one of you gents lead us out of here? I don't want to bother you guys by getting lost and wandering around before I find my way out." I was already feeling a little better.

A couple of Gristle's followers escorted us out a different way than we came. We emerged from a manhole a half a block down from my car. I can't tell you how big of a sigh of relief I let out. I even felt the stripper relax a little in my arms when she saw the moon and the streetlights.

I tossed them my now useless Maglite. "That piece of shit needs new batteries. Enjoy, kids."

CHAPTER 8

Well, now I had the book that everyone wanted, and an ugly, traumatized stripper that no one did.

She seemed like she was in pretty bad shape, both mentally and physically. I can only imagine the kinds of torment that the Munchkins had been subjecting her to for God knows how long down here in these tunnels. I had probably seen her at Camelot the last time I was in there, which was a couple months prior, so that didn't really narrow down the time when they might have snatched her. She could have been down there for two days or two months, no way of knowing unless I asked her, but I wasn't quite ready to go there. The Munchkins had clearly used some of whatever kind of magic they possessed on her. I remembered her as a woman taller than I was. Now he was shrunken almost a foot, and her face and body were warped or twisted somehow, but still pretty much recognizable. No way anyone would ever take a look at her in her present shape and think she was attractive, much less sexy like she used to be. She was homely, bordering on the ugly, now. Nothing fifty grand in plastic surgery wouldn't fix, but she'd never be what anyone would call beautiful again, that was for sure.

We had both made it out of the tunnels alive somehow, though, and that was what was important right now. Plus I had the book. We were both covered in filth and needed a long, hot shower to remove the dirt and shit and whatever else was caked on us. It wasn't going to be as easy to scrub off the memory of what we had seen— and the stripper experienced—down here.

"You're safe now. I'll help you and take you away from them. They won't hurt you again, I promise. What's your name? Everyone just calls me Augustino," I said to her when we finally made it back to my car. I wanted to get her inside before one of DC's finest noticed me with a filthy, naked chick. I didn't need to get hauled in for rape or something.

She wasn't talking. Not that I'm surprised. I didn't want to traumatize her any more than she already had been. She was practically catatonic as it was, just letting me lead her along by the arm.

I spread a couple of beach towels I keep in the car down so we wouldn't get too much filth on the seats. It was inevitable though. After I helped her get seated in the car and buckled her in, I started the car and heard her say softly, "My name is Sarah."

I turned toward her and patted her hand. She didn't flinch *too* much. "It's nice to meet you, Sarah. I can take you home or to the hospital, or you can stay with me for a while until you get better, whatever you like. What do you want to do?" In a weird way, I didn't really want to take her to the hospital. While I know she probably really did need to be checked out by a doctor, I didn't want her to get committed to a mental institution for the rest of her life because she wouldn't stop ranting about being kidnapped by a pack of feral midgets living in tunnels underground who shrank her and made her ugly.

"I don't want anyone to see me like this . . . I don't want to go home either. That's where they . . . they . . . ."

"It's OK, Sarah, we don't have to go back to your place, let's just head back to my place. You can rest up there as long as you want and get cleaned up and just relax and feel safe for a while." She nodded and cried silently.

"Do you have any cigarettes?" she asked abruptly after a few minutes. "I could really use a cigarette." I didn't, not being a smoker, so I stopped at a convenience store and picked her up a pack and a lighter. I had to help her get it lit; her hands were shaking, and she couldn't seem to get it going.

I headed back to my apartment. It's a smallish one-bedroom in Mount Pleasant. The place is a dump, but it's quiet, the neighbors leave me alone, and the landlord doesn't raise the rent on me. I've lived there for years and years, and the place looks it, but it suits me fine. Typical mismatched and second-hand bachelor furniture, trash that no one nagged me to take out, small herds of dust bunnies under and behind, well, everything. Plus, my own books fill the place…double-stacked on my bookshelves, in piles on the floor, tucked away in the closets. Some science fiction, fantasy, horror, lots of crime, a few scattered copies of the young adult series he had enjoyed as a kid. Nothing valuable—certainly nothing worth twenty grand, and nothing the Bookworm would ever want—but they were mine and I loved them.

When we got back to my apartment, I wrapped Sarah in a towel and helped her inside. I gave her some water and multivitamins first, then started making her some food. God knows how long it had been since she had last had a decent meal. I can't cook for shit, but I can pop a Hungry Man TV dinner into the microwave with the best of 'em. She ate that TV dinner like it was the best meal she'd ever eaten. By the time she was done, I could tell she was starting to doze off. She wanted to take a shower first though, and I can't say that I blamed her. Dear God, she was filthy. Even dirtier than I was, and that was saying something. She took a long, long hot shower. When she was done I helped her into the bedroom and tucked her in with a couple extra blankets. I checked in on her a few minutes later, and she was already out like a light.

I needed a shower and a long winter's nap pretty badly myself, but I figured I'd check on my answering machine and give Jack a quick call to let him know how I was doing. I wasn't planning on calling the Bookworm until the next morning, because I knew he'd want me to bring the book over right away. No way I felt like doing that. I was beat . . . and I didn't think the girl should be left alone right now. He could stew until the morning. The book would be fine right here with me for the night. Besides, I wanted a little time alone with the book to savor it.

I checked the answering machine. One message: "Hello, Augustino, this is the Fat Man. I assume my infamy precedes me. In any case, I have your partner, and I want the book you should now have in your possession. Here is your friend." Jack came on the line. "Look, kid, whatever the Bookworm is paying you for the book, it's not worth it. These guys are serious. Just do what the Fat Man says so I can get the hell out of here." The Fat Man came back on. "I'm willing to trade Mr. Scanlon here for the book. If you're interested, bring the book to the top of the Exorcist Stairs in Georgetown at three p.m. tomorrow. Park at the gas station at the base of the stairs and walk up. Come alone. Involving the authorities is the quickest way to get your partner killed, as is telling the Bookworm or anyone else. Have a wonderful evening, and I'll see you tomorrow." I could hear the smile in that fat fuck's voice.

Fuck. This was not good. Not good at all.

CHAPTER 9

Michael had been looking for a new job for six months. He was tired of being a waiter and living the whole restaurant lifestyle: wake up mid-afternoon still a little hung over, throw on some clothes, start work at 4 or 4:30, work until close, drink at an after-hours bar for another couple hours with other waitstaff, then stumble home and sleep. He needed a change. Something exciting, something at least a little intellectually challenging.

Michael had been grabbing the paper every day for the past week and studying the classifieds, but nothing looked even vaguely appealing. Not that many jobs would even take someone with a G.E.D. anyway. Then he saw the ad from Scanlon and Associates, Private Investigators.

That actually sounds pretty interesting. Never thought of that, but it might be fun. What the hell? Michael thought.

So he called the number listed in the ad and set up an interview for the next day with the gruff-sounding old dude who answered.

Michael was fairly unimpressed with the low-rent office at U Street, but he figured beggars can't be choosers. Plus, it wasn't like he was applying to be the next James Bond. Michael knew he had to set his expectations realistically. He was dreading having to go back to the restaurant that night.

Michael went inside to find himself in a cramped, run-down office with beat-up furniture. A black-and-white TV was blaring in the corner, its picture hard to make out behind the snow. A balding guy with a greasy comb-over, late middle-age, in a rumpled suit was sitting behind a desk reading the newspaper with his feet propped up on the desk. The man didn't look up when Michael came in.

"I'm Michael Augustino. I'm here for the interview."

"Oh, yeah, hi, how's it going?" the man said, putting the paper down and standing up. They shook hands across the desk. "I'm Jack Scanlon. Just clear the crap off that chair and have a seat."

Michael moved a pile of paperwork and file folders off the chair and onto the desk and sat down gingerly. The seat cushion was split down the middle and at least one of the chair's legs seemed a little wobbly. Michael warned himself not to make any sudden movements.

"You want some coffee? There should still be some in the pot I made this morning." Michael declined with a headshake.

"Jesus, you're young," Jack said.

Michael didn't know how to reply to that, so he didn't. Nothing he could do about that now, except wait to get old.

"OK, let me tell you about the job, then you tell me about yourself if the job doesn't scare you off. You'd be working as my assistant, and I'd train you to be a private investigator. You'd start out as my assistant, kind of an apprentice, really. I'll teach you everything I know. I do divorce cases, insurance fraud, background checks, missing persons cases, that sort of thing. Pretty much whenever someone wants to find out something that someone else is trying to conceal, they come to me. You'll get your private detective license here in DC. I'll help you with that, it's incredibly easy. Just a form and a licensing fee, pretty much."

"Now, I'm not going to lie to you. The job isn't all that glamorous, and you'll probably never be rich and famous. A lot of the work is fairly dry, mundane, boring shit. Like sitting in a car for hours on end waiting for a guy to come out of a motel room with his girlfriend so you can take some pictures. That kind of crap. Hours and hours of boredom and a few minutes of excitement. And you're going to have to help me get the office organized a bit. It's hard to believe, I know, but I've let the organizational side of things fall by the wayside a bit. I've gotta tell you, though, as long as I've been doing this, it's still fun. Naturally, I prefer the cases that are a little more interesting, a little more out of the ordinary, you'll see what I mean if you stick around long enough, but they all have their moments. Never once in my entire career have I hated my job."

"If that doesn't sound like something you'd be interested in, hey, let me know. No hard feelings, and that way neither one of us wastes our time."

"No, in all honesty," Michael replied, surprising himself with his enthusiasm, "that sounds great. Even the boring parts. I have to say, I'm impressed that you've never once hated your job or dreaded coming in to work. That's exactly the kind of job I'm looking for. Something that's going to make me want to keep coming back for more."

"OK, I like what I'm hearing. Why don't you tell me about yourself?" asked Jack.

"Well, like I said, my name is Michael Augustino. I was born and raised here in DC, so I know the city like the back of my hand. I finished up with high school a few years ago, and I've been on my own ever since. I worked a few odd jobs when I first graduated, then I got into the restaurant industry. I started off bussing tables for a while, then I got into being a waiter. I've been doing that at a couple restaurants in Adams Morgan for about the last three years, but I'm pretty sick of it at this point. It's mind numbingly boring, and I'm looking for something a little more intellectually stimulating."

"So what do you like to do when you're not waiting tables?"

"I know it's a little geeky, but my main hobby is reading. I'm a voracious reader and will read anything you put in front of me. I'm a big fan of crime fiction, among other things, so that's why your ad really intrigued me. For some reason it never really crossed my mind that I could work as a private investigator until I saw your ad."

Jack nodded, looking deep in thought.

"What's your background, Mr. Scanlon, if you don't mind me asking? How did you get into the P.I. business?" Michael asked.

"Well, a buddy of mine offered me a job helping out in his detective business up in Baltimore after I got out of the Navy. I did a little surveillance work for him, a little missing persons work, that sort of thing, off and on for a couple years, then decided to start my own business. I wanted to be my own boss, so I moved down to DC, set up shop and never looked back."

They chit-chatted for a while, getting to know each other a little better. Jack got up and refilled his coffee cup with some of the thick, room temperature coffee in the pot.

"So, you got any other questions for me?" Jack asked.

Michael looked around the dingy office. "Yeah, just one: where are the associates?" Jack just stared at him for a moment. "The sign on the door and the ad in the *Post* said it was Jack Scanlon *and Associates.*"

"Ah, a smartass, I see. I'm probably going to regret this, but do you want the job or what?"

The money Jack was offering wasn't much better than a decent hourly rate on a weekday night at the restaurant. Michael knew he would never get rich by living the "glamorous" life of a private investigator, but Jack seemed like a decent guy. He was dreading going back to the restaurant anyway. Surly, demanding customers, poor tips, a dick for a manager, and dimwitted waitresses had long ago lost their appeal.

"Yeah, sure. I'd love the job."

"OK, you're hired. Now I have an 'associate.' Happy? I assume you can start pretty much immediately?"

And just like that, Michael started working with Jack.

#

Michael spent most of his first couple weeks cleaning up the office and getting the place organized. Getting Jack's case files organized and filed away took more than a week by themselves. As Michael would go through each file, he would quiz Jack for more information on each case, and Jack would talk for hours on end about the minutiae of some of the cases. Michael began to wonder if maybe he had been hired because Jack wanted someone to talk to as much as he wanted an assistant. Whichever the case, Michael was fascinated by Jack's tales. Jack had one locked cabinet full of case files he wouldn't let Michael into. Michael basically brushed it off and didn't get offended. He assumed the cases were sensitive in some way. He wondered if Jack would ever trust him enough to let him read *all* the case files.

Michael learned fairly quickly that Jack had a thing for hanging out in cheap hotel bars and trying to pick up bored businesswomen and frumpy housewives looking for some excitement. He liked to talk about his past sexual exploits, which initially made Michael vaguely uncomfortable. Eventually though, Michael became immune to it, and nothing Jack said could phase him. He learned more than he ever thought possible about good scotch and horse racing (Jack was a reasonably heavy drinker, though he never appeared drunk, Michael soon learned, and he seemed to spend an inordinate amount of time at the Pimlico racetrack in Baltimore).

And, almost incidentally, along the way Michael learned the ins and outs of the private investigation business: how to find people, places, and things that didn't want to be found. Jack was a damn fine detective when he cared about the case, and he was more than happy to share the fine points of detective work.

Michael's first real case with Jack gave him the "bug" to want to stick with the detective business (and with Jack, in particular) came after about two months on the job. The case involved a big-time lobbyist's cheating wife, her girlfriend, their pimp, a blackmail scheme, and a stolen briefcase full of $100 bills and vibrators. Michael had never experienced anything more exciting than helping Jack track down all the players, figure out what was going on, recover the stolen briefcase, and explain to the lobbyist what was really going on with his wife and why she wasn't coming back to him.

Jack warned him after they finished the case and collected their fee: "They usually aren't that exciting, kid. I know that was a fun one, but I've gotta tell you, those are the unusual ones."

Michael didn't care, though; he wasn't even listening. He was just staring at his paycheck—with a generous bonus—and thinking about what a wild ride it had been, and grinning from ear to ear. He couldn't wait for the next client to walk through the door.

Gradually, over time, Michael learned that Jack also liked to delve into cases that were more than a little weird. The smallest hint of oddity or facts that didn't quite add up or couldn't be easily explained intrigued Jack. The point was brought home to Michael about six months after he started working with Jack when Jack introduced him to an old client: a man named Mort who claimed to be: (1) a sorcerer; and (2) tormented by the spirit of his dead wife. Jack took it all in stride, not even blinking, and asked all the right questions at the appropriate times. Michael sat in his chair dumbfounded, not saying a word. After Mort had thanked them for taking the case, paid his retainer, and left, Michael finally managed to close his gaping mouth and ask Jack, "So he was crazy, right? He's some kind of nutjob who comes in every so often, pays you some money, you pretend to fix his ghost problem, and that's that?"

"Well . . . no. Not exactly, kid. You see, he's not actually crazy. I've been doing odd jobs for Mort for years, and he really is a sorcerer. A minor one, you can be sure about that—there are guys around town who eat chumps like him for breakfast—but he's an honest-to-God sorcerer."

Michael burst out laughing.

"No, seriously, Jack. What's his deal?"

"I wasn't kidding, kid," Jack said gravely. "I probably should've told you about this stuff before now, but I wasn't sure you were ready."

Michael had known Jack long enough to realize that Jack wasn't pulling his leg on this one. "You honestly mean to tell me that he really is a sorcerer? And you believe that? Have you seen him cast a spell?"

Jack gave Michael an even stare. "I've seen a lot more than just that. Look, I can tell you don't believe me. It's only natural that you're skeptical. I would be too in your shoes. OK, just promise me that you'll keep an open mind about the case, keep your mouth shut, play along, follow my lead, and don't be surprised if you see something that changes your mind."

The next day, Jack and Michael went over to Mort's house, had dinner with him, and stayed the night. Every night for the last two weeks, Mort told then, the spirit of his dead wife returned to visit and, in general, torment him. Flying around the house, through walls and doors, dropping the temperature of the room, throwing things around and knocking things over, saying mean, nasty, evil things; you know, the usual things that ghosts are said to do. She apparently liked to chastise him in particular for ruining the good name of Mort's best friend, Sal the Crumb, another minor sorcerer who Jack had also known for years. Apparently, Mort and Sal had recently had a major falling out over some minor disagreement, as old, stubborn men are wont to do. In retaliation for Sal doing whatever it was that he had supposedly done, Mort had gone around disparaging Sal's "good name."

"We've been pals for years, but about two or three months ago, we had an argument. A bad one. I don't want to go into what it was about. In hindsight, it was stupid. You know how it goes. But Sal said some very hurtful things, and I told some of our mutual acquaintances a few things about the real Sal the Crumb, just to teach him a lesson, and he didn't like that. I didn't say anything that wasn't true, though."

It rapidly became clear to Jack and Michael that Sal was probably the prime suspect behind the new haunting, though Mort vehemently denied the possibly. "No, guys, I swear to you, it really is the spirit of my wife, Mary. There's no way that Sal could be involved in this. He wouldn't do that to me. I swear to you, she's come back from the dead!"

But Jack was not to be dissuaded. So they went to visit Sal the Crumb and find out what, if anything, he knew about the haunting. Sal lived in a dingy little basement apartment in the shadow of Capitol Hill. He answered the door in a coffee-stained terrycloth bathrobe when they rang the bell.

"Hey, Jack, how's it going? Long time no see. Say, who's the new kid?"

Jack made the introductions, and Sal invited them in for coffee. They sat down on a dingy old brown leather couch and sipped their coffee (Michael just had some water) out of dirty mugs. Jack got down to business after a few minutes of reminiscing about the "good old days" and what the DC occult scene had been like during the seventies. It sounded to Michael like it involved a lot of drinking and music by bands he had never heard of.

"I'm going to lay it all out on the table," Jack finally said. "We're here about Mort's recent problems with the spirit of his dead wife. We know that Mort and you had a falling out not too long ago. We know that he's been going around to your old pals and saying some pretty hateful things about you, smearing your name around. That's shitty. He shouldn't have done that. But the poor old fart doesn't deserve to be haunted by his wife's ghost every night for the rest of his life. Now, I'm not going to come right out and accuse you of anything, but I remember you as a pretty decent necromancer back in the day, Sal. Hell, I've seen you conjure a ghost or two, myself. It's not an incredible stretch for me to put two and two together and begin to wonder if maybe you're not involved somehow in what's been happening to Mort."

Sal pondered this for a while, staring morosely into his coffee mug. "Look, guys, I want you to know, the 'spirit' who's been visiting Mort isn't really his dead wife's spirit. I wouldn't do that to a guy, especially an old friend like Mort. Besides, his wife Lily was always real nice to me. No way I'd make her spirit return from the land of the dead—I know what it does to them. She's gone to her eternal reward, no way I'd bring her back. The 'spirit' is really just an illusion I've been conjuring up to harass him. It's not really a dead person's spirit."

"Now, I guess Mort has pretty much already gotten what he deserved, but, dammit—Mort has got to stop telling people I'm a hack and a loser, and all the rest of the crap he's been saying about me. All a man's really got is his reputation, and Mort is ruining mine. I couldn't just let that go by. You understand, don't you, Jack? You'd have done the same thing I did, if it had happened to you. But if you get Mort to agree to stop spreading nasty rumors about me, I'll let bygones be bygones. If he apologizes to me—and really means it, mind you—I'll come over to his place and dispel the curse I laid on him."

"Sounds fair to me, Sal," Jack responded. "That's all I can ask."

Michael waited until they had left Sal's place until he expressed his complete and utter disbelief. "Jack, enough's enough. I mean, I appreciate the fact that you're just humoring the old farts, but come on! What was that shit back there about seeing him conjure up ghosts twenty years ago? You can't be serious!"

All Jack would say was, "Keep an open mind, kid. You just might learn something."

So they went back to Mort's place to try to convince Mort to apologize and thereby mediate a truce between the two old sorcerers. It took Jack more than an hour at his persuasive best to get Mort to come around. Eventually, Jack was able to convince Mort to forgive Sal, apologize to him for tarnishing his good name, and kiss and make friends again. Michael was frankly amazed that Jack was able to get the old coot to agree to make friends again. Jack gave Sal a call and told him to come over to Mort's place to accept the apology and cancel the haunting curse.

Sal told Jack he'd be over shortly, but it wasn't going to be quite that easy to get rid of the curse. Sal told Jack that the curse was basically on auto-pilot, and he would have to wait until the "spirit" appeared again before he could get rid of it.

When Michael heard this, he rolled his eyes, but was looking forward to seeing what crazy mumbo-jumbo the old fart would trot out to end the "haunting."

When Sal arrived, Mort took him aside, they talked quietly in the next room for a long while, and eventually Mort apologized for blackening Sal's good name, Sal apologized for the "haunting," and they hugged. Very touching. Mort appeared very relieved to hear that it was all an illusion, and not actually the spirit of his wife.

They all sat around drinking Irish coffee—Coke in the case of Michael—laughing, and carrying on like the old friends they were in Mort's living room until midnight, when Mort said the "spirit" of his dead wife would appear.

Sure enough, at the stroke of midnight on Mort's old grandfather clock, something started happening. The room became unnaturally still and quiet. There was a sudden tension in the air, and all the hairs on the back of Michael's neck stood up. He blinked a couple times, and rubbed his eyes, but, sure enough, something was slowly materializing in the center of the room. It looked like a cloud of thin gray smoke gradually coalescing into the shape of a woman, floating about a foot off the ground. Michael was so startled by her sudden appearance that he dropped his glass, spilling soda all over his lap. Only Jack's firm grip kept him from bolting off the couch. "Just watch, kid, you might just learn something."

Sal set his coffee down on the end table, while Jack and Mort both settled back in their seats and continued to sip at their coffee occasionally, looking interested but not concerned. Michael was as nonplussed by their reactions to the apparition as he was the apparition itself.

The smoky woman began to speak in a breathy whisper, "Mort, you have betrayed your oldest friend. You have betrayed our marriage vows. You have—"

Sal cut her off, speaking in a commanding voice: "Chimera, I am your creator. You will obey me. I alone gave you life. I alone can dispel you. I command you to begone. Begone I say!" As Sal spoke, wisps began coming off the spirit, drifting off toward the ceiling and disappearing. Holes began to appear in it. Michael could now actually see through the spirit; he saw the curio cabinet across the room containing a lifetime of old lady kitsch through it.

And just like that, the apparition faded to nothingness and was gone.

Sal turned to Mort and said, "Old buddy, I'm sorry I did that to you. You deserved better than that."

Mort hopped up, saying, "And I'm sorry too, Sal. I shouldn't have said all those things just because we had a stupid argument." The two men embraced, gently patting each other on the back.

Jack turned to Michael. "Well, kid, what do you think? I'd say our work here is done." Michael couldn't quite get a reply out. He dumbly nodded and slurped down what was left of his Coke.

The two old sorcerers thanked them, and Sal agreed to pay half Jack and Michael's fee, promising to bring it by the office in the morning.

When Jack and Michael got out to Jack's car, he asked Michael if he was OK, since Michael still hadn't said a word.

"Yeah . . . I'm OK. Jack? Question for you. What the hell happened back there?"

"What do you mean, 'what happened?' You saw it with your own eyes. Sal had cursed Mort because of one of those ridiculous arguments that old friends sometimes have, then we convinced Sal to end the curse. A textbook case, really." Jack looked smug.

"OK, that's what I thought happened. Just checking."

Neither of them said anything for a few stoplights.

"So are you OK dealing with the occasional case like that, kid? I mean, most of them are still going to be divorce cases and missing persons, and all that mundane shit, but occasionally they're a little more . . . interesting, shall we say. You're not too freaked out about it?"

Michael thought about it for a few seconds. "Freaked out? Freaked out? Are you kidding? That was the weirdest thing I've ever seen. It was awesome! I loved it! Can't wait until the next freaky case we get."

Which was a significantly better reaction than Jack had feared he might have.

After that, Michael and Jack grew increasingly close. They spent many of their off-duty hours together, drinking, playing cards, or just shooting the shit. Michael grew to enjoy Jack's "weird cases," and he prompted Jack to introduce him to a variety of other local magical practitioners. While Michael never grew to be as comfortable as Jack around magic, he found himself strangely drawn to it and relished the "weird" cases as welcome breaks from the usual assortment of mundane cases the two usually dealt with.

They had been working together a few years when Michael started dating a wild, feisty little Korean-American bartender named Jenny, the one and only woman who broke his heart. After Michael had been dating Jenny for a couple months, Jack said something he knew he shouldn't to Michael. Jack had been looking uncomfortable all morning, and Michael knew that Jack had something awkward to say. Michael had almost been wondering if he was about to be fired. Jack broke out of the blue. "I'm going to say something I know you don't want to hear. I shouldn't say it, but I can't stand by and not say anything. Watch out for Jenny, kid. She's trouble. She's going to cut your heart out of your chest and shit all over it. I can see it coming a mile away. I've seen it a million times before. She's a man-eater. I know that sounds harsh, but I've seen it all and—"

"Jesus, Jack, you're not my father!"

Jack didn't say anything for a long while. "I know I'm not." Michael had never seen Jack unable to look him in the eye before.

"Just because you can't make any relationships work doesn't mean I can't! Things are going great with Jenny! She's incredible! I love her, and she loves me! We're perfect together!"

Jack didn't reply, and he didn't look at Michael either. Michael took off after a couple minutes, not saying a word, and didn't come back to the office for a week. When he did, Jack greeted him like old times, never remarking on his absence or Jenny again. It was the only argument they had ever had. Jack didn't say anything a few months later when Michael told him that Jenny had broken up with him over the weekend. They both moved on.

Over the years, they worked for almost everyone in the local DC occult underground at one time or another. Michael got to know all the heavy hitters like Nocturne, the Stone King, and the Separated Woman, as well as some of the small fry wannabes like Wriggler, the Scab, Mort and Sal, and everyone in between. Michael learned that, despite his rumpled appearance, Jack had managed to build a sizable reputation as a troubleshooter and detective among the local freaks.

They had settled into a very comfortable relationship: part mentor-protégé, part father-son, part drinking buddies, and part best friends. They saw each other almost every day of the week, usually spending a good chunk of the day working on a case together or just talking. Being "manly" men, neither discussed their relationship, of course, but if pressed, both Michael and Jack would have privately admitted that they had never had a friendship as close as the one they shared.

CHAPTER 10

So I didn't really have much of a choice. Jack was, well, *Jack*. He meant . . . a lot to me. I had no idea where the Fat Man might be holding Jack, and while I could probably track him down, the chance of me finding them and staging some kind of half-assed rescue attempt (or even just calling in the cops) between now and three p.m. was pretty much nil. I could keep the book, get the money from the Bookworm, and live happily ever after knowing that no one would be summoning some unspeakable monster from another dimension to rule the world. However, I would always know that I had let my only real friend die. And probably die in some horrible, unspeakable fashion. Or I could walk into what was probably an ambush tomorrow and try to get my partner back, knowing that even if I did, a maniac who was willing to use it now had the book.

Jesus. What a fucking choice.

No real choice at all, I realized after a couple minutes. I had to at least try to get Jack back alive. And that meant trading the book for him. Yeah, the book was worth twenty grand, and if what the Bookworm had told me was true, it would be *really* bad for a scumbag like the Fat Man to get his hands on it, but that's the way it goes sometimes. Besides, once I had Jack back, we could both do our damnedest to get the book back from the Fat Man later and stop whatever he had planned (oh and incidentally still end up earning the Bookworm's twenty grand). No way I could call the cops for help, that was an unspoken but sacrosanct rule in the occult underground. So no cops, no normals to be brought in under any circumstances.

And I didn't really know anyone already clued-in who I'd trust to help me with this. Jack was pretty much it on that score. Which left me on my own.

#

I had a hell of a time falling asleep, despite the fact that I was exhausted. I couldn't stop thinking about Jack and what was going to go down with the Fat Man the next day, plus I knew that the instant I actually fell asleep, the next thing I knew I'd be waking up with nightmares.

I grabbed a couple blankets and turned my couch into a bed since Sarah had the bedroom. My couch is perfect for sleeping, I can't tell you how many wonderful naps I've had on it. I figured I might as well try a little "light reading" to help me fall asleep, so I opened the book's leather case, pulled it out and figured I'd give it a try and see if I could figure out why everyone wanted the damn thing so badly. The book was printed in that archaic type you've seen in the history books that they used back then. Not exactly easy on the eyes. I quickly found myself reading and rereading the same passages because I couldn't understand a word I was reading. Yeah, I knew what all the words meant individually (OK, I knew what *most* of the words meant individually), but I couldn't make heads or tails of what good ol' Ben was trying to say. I flipped to the back third of the book where I had noticed the diagrams and line drawings. Those I could understand a little easier. To my untrained eye, they looked like a series of pentagrams and similar geometric patterns. From what I could tell, those were the various symbols required to summon/contact Tiamat. But hell, what do I know? I'm not even a novice sorcerer. Jack had picked up more about magic rituals over the years, so he could probably have puzzled out a bit more than I could, but I suspected this stuff would have been beyond him as well. Guess it really was only useful to a trained sorcerer. No wonder the Munchkins had been willing to trade it away, after they had seen that they had stolen something completely incomprehensible to them.

By this point, I had relaxed enough that I was able to fall into a light, fitful sleep. I kept waking up, checking on the book, making sure it was still there. I nearly had a heart attack about four in the morning because when I woke to check on the book, it wasn't on the coffee table right in front of me, where I was sure I had left it. I sat bolt upright, my heart racing a mile a minute, then I noticed the book had fallen on the floor. Guess I had knocked it off the table with a flailing arm when I had that last nightmare. Yes, I had nightmares all night, just like I had every night for the last week. No, I don't want to talk about them.

Sarah was still asleep when I got up, pretty peacefully by the looks of it when I poked my head into the bedroom to check on her. I figured rest was probably the best thing for her at this point. I got her a glass of water, moved the books stacked on the bedside table, and put the water down in easy reach of her when she did finally wake up. She never even knew I was there. I left some breakfast food and lunch-type things out on the counter, then left her a note that I was going to be gone for most of the day, but that she should make herself at home. I'd have liked to stuck around to make sure that she was OK when she finally woke up, but I just didn't have the time, unfortunately. Jack needed me more right now. I had a quick breakfast then headed out the door.

I figured I'd head to the office this morning and grab the handgun that Jack keeps in the top drawer of his desk. Now normally, I'm not a big fan of guns. Sure, I have a shotgun at home that I keep under the bed in case some asshole breaks into the apartment, but I never carry around a handgun. You can't really in DC, unless you're a criminal. Any law-abiding citizen with a handgun in DC gets locked up if they get caught. I had spent a couple nights in the DC jail over the years, and I had little to no interest in repeating the experience. I also had a neat little folding knife I kept clipped to the inside of my right front pocket, the blade-length within a hair's width of being illegal. I could open the knife and pop the blade into position with just a flick of the wrist. Oh, and of course, I've got my wits. Damn. Guess that was going to have to be enough.

I grabbed the book, still in the leather case the Munchkins had given to me and headed out to my car. When I got to the office, it was neatly locked up, nothing amiss. No sign of a struggle, and it didn't look like anyone had taken anything or rifled through any of the files. Guess they probably snatched Jack from his apartment or out on the street somewhere. His pistol was right where I expected to find it. I made sure it was loaded, the safety was on, and I tucked it into my waistband in the small of my back. I could deal with accidentally shooting myself in the ass cheek a lot easier than I could deal with getting a nut shot off.

I wasn't exactly overwhelmed with joy at meeting the Fat Man at the Exorcist Stairs in Georgetown. They are an immensely tall, narrow set of steps in Georgetown that connect Prospect Street with M Street at 36th Street. If you've seen *The Exorcist*, you've seen these stairs. The priest throws himself down them. Very spooky shit. Every time I've driven past them on M St., I've always gotten a little chill thinking about that scene. Perfect place for a set-up. No choice in the matter though. I had made my bed, now I was going to have to sleep in it.

#

I parked at the gas station at the base of the stairs a few minutes before three, just like a good little boy, and began trudging upward. Seemed like there were hundreds of steps, and I was a little winded by the time I got to the top. Jesus, I wouldn't want to fall down these. Not many people around on a cold, blustery Sunday afternoon in Georgetown. Clear, bright blue sky, though. Pretty, almost. I immediately saw the Fat Man and Little Boy standing there at the top, Little Boy with a firm grip on Jack. Jack's hands were clasped in front of him with a jacket covering them. I assume he was handcuffed. He didn't look so good. He's not exactly a spring chicken and being kidnapped and probably roughed up wasn't doing wonders for him.

The Fat Man waddled over to me. "Glad you decided to play it smart, Augustino." He was a few inches shorter than me, probably 5'8" or so, reddish hair starting to go gray, raggedy goatee. He was, well, there's no way around it, morbidly obese. The blue track suit he had squeezed himself into was taut over his belly, and his arms and legs rubbed up against the rest of his body when he moved. I could hear him breathing heavily through his nose. Bet that fucker didn't walk up those stairs.

"Is that the book, there?" He pointed to the leather case.

"Yeah it is, but we need to talk some before we make the trade. First, I want to know what you plan to do with the book. Second, I want to be *very* clear on how we trade the book for Jack. I don't want any tricks, Fat Man. All I want is Jack back. In exchange, you get your precious book."

"First," the Fat Man said, poking my chest, "It's none of your goddamn business what I choose to do with the book. You've lost. I'll do whatever I want to with the book. You have no say in the matter.

"Second—" he started to poke me in the chest again but I grabbed his finger and twisted it, viciously. No one pokes me in the chest twice. His prissy lips twisted into a grimace and he backed off a step, shaking his hand to get it out of my grasp. "*Second*, you'll get Jack back once I have the book in my hands, and I'm seated safely in my car. Jack will walk with us to the car, then we'll let him go as we get inside." I didn't like this, but I had little choice in the matter. Besides, I knew I could run faster than these two tubs of lard. And I could always shoot out their tires or something. (Yeah, right. I could probably hit the car from ten or fifteen feet away, but the tires? Forget about it.)

"OK, Fat Man, we'll play it your way. I'll hand you the book, you and Fat Boy walk back to the car with Jack, and he goes free when you get there. That's all there is to it, right?"

He nodded. I handed the book over. He stepped back a couple steps toward Jack and Little Boy and took it out of the case. He flipped through it, stopping to read a bit every few pages. He looked like he was entranced, staring at some of the diagrams. They were impenetrable to me, but he knew a hell of a lot more about this stuff than I did.

He appeared to be satisfied with the book, slipping it back in the case and wedging it under one arm. "Before we hand your good buddy Jack back over to you, I think there's someone else you should see, Augustino," Fat Man cackled. Little Boy started giggling almost uncontrollably. He didn't let go of Jack though. Fat Man half-turned and beckoned to someone sitting in a silver Ford Explorer parked nearby. The door opened and she got out, walked over. It was unmistakably her, though we hadn't seen each other in thirteen years: my sister, Angela.

Jesus, she looked like more of a tramp than ever. The years had not been particularly kind to Angela. Looked like she had been ridden hard and put away wet. When I last saw her, Angela was a typical cute little sixteen year old Italian girl. Long black curly hair, a bad temper, and a filthy mouth. There were wrinkles around her eyes and mouth now, and she was way too tan. Her dark hair was streaked with blonde highlights. Some blind guy must have put them in for her. She ought to try washing that rat's nest once a while too. Shit, I don't mean to be as catty as I remember her being, but for a twenty-nine year old, she could easily have passed for forty. I'm probably a little biased though, hating her like I do.

She walked over to me, getting just inside my personal space comfort zone. "Hello, Michael. Long time, no see. Missed me? Last time I saw you, you were scurrying out of the house with your tail between your legs."

"Last time I saw you, Angie, I thought you were dead." She hates to be called Angie.

"I almost was, thanks to you, you bastard." She pulled down her top some, exposing some ugly red scars on her chest and upper arm.

"Lovely as ever. Actually, I can't say I've missed you much, sis. Nice to see you've taken after your mother." I refused to acknowledge that bitch as my mother too. And I *really* didn't want to think too much about the fact that Angela was still alive. And right here in front of me. "Can't say that I'm surprised that you've gotten yourself caught up with these low-lives either."

"Caught up with them?" she laughed. "You've gotta be shitting me. These two slobs would still be at home stuffing their fat faces if it wasn't for me. *I'm* the one who turned them on to the book."

"Look, Angie—"

"Don't call me that! My name is Streghina now. Just like mother was Strega, I am Streghina." Oh God, she was even crazier than I thought. Our mother always called herself the Strega, Italian for witch, and now Angela was calling herself the 'Little Witch.'

Our relationship had started to sour when I walked in on her giving her boyfriend a blowjob when she was fourteen, and she threatened to kill me if I told anyone. I really don't like people threatening to kill me, even if they *are* family. Especially if they're family. I know kids say a lot of shit they don't mean, but she and I both knew, deep down, that she meant every word of it. She really *was* willing to kill me. It went downhill from there.

"OK, OK, I got it. You're Streghina. Like I was about to say: look, you win. You and the fatsos wanted the book. I found it, brought it here, and gave it to you. I just want my partner back. I don't give a shit about the book. It's obviously caused me a lot more trouble than it's worth. I don't want anything more to do with it. Fatso has the book in hand, so just let Jack go, we'll let bygones be bygones, and we can go back to ignoring each other's existence. The past is the past. It's all water under the bridge now. What happened between us was a very long time ago and has nothing to do with the book or Jack or anything else. Let's just try to move on with our lives. No hard feelings."

"Oh there are still some very hard feelings, *Michael*," she hissed. "I haven't forgotten how we parted, you son of a bitch." I ignored the irony of what she just called her precious mother.

"You killed our mother, you bastard!" Angela screamed in that shrill, nasal voice I remembered so fondly. "I'm going to make you pay for that. I'm going to make you wish you had never been born. I'm going to take away everything you ever cared about, just like you did to me!" Without hesitating in the least, she ran back toward Fat Man, Little Boy, and Jack. She pulled a knife out of somewhere, grabbed Jack's hair, reached over with the knife, and cut Jack's throat from ear to ear. Just like that. Couldn't have taken more than three seconds all told. Blood gushed everywhere. Jack started to make these horrible, high-pitched wheezing sounds. Angela pushed him down, knocking him out of Little Boy's grip. Jack fell to the ground right at the top of the stairs, and for a brief second I thought he was going to tumble all the way down. I was dimly aware that Angela and the others had run back to the car and were starting to pull off. I couldn't believe my eyes. What the fuck had just happened? How did things spin out of control so goddamn fast?

CHAPTER 11

Before I go on, there's something you need to know: she's right. I killed my mother when I was eighteen. Before you get too judgmental, you should know that I had no choice. She and my sister had just cut my father's heart out.

#

Michael walked up the front steps of his family's rowhouse and opened the door quietly. It was Michael's senior year, and he was skipping afternoon classes again. He didn't want his mother to hear him coming home early. Not that she cared much, but there would be a yelling match, and she would find some way to get back at him for disobeying her. She always did. His plan was to just slip quietly upstairs and go into his room and read and listen to his headphones for a couple hours until it was time for him to actually be home from school. He had done it plenty of times before, and as long as his bitchy little sister Angela didn't discover him, everything would be fine. Everything was going according to plan until he passed through the kitchen on his way to the stairs and heard the sound of voices coming up from the basement. The doorway to the basement was in the kitchen. Normally whenever Michael's mother was down there doing whatever it was that she did down there, she had the door shut and locked from the inside. Not today though. The door was ajar, and he could clearly hear his mother's voice along with his sister's. They were both chanting things in unison. He couldn't quite make out what they were saying. It was in some weird, foreign language. Not Italian, either. Michael knew enough Italian to get a sense of it, and they definitely weren't chanting in Italian or Latin. It was some deep, guttural sounding language that came from the back of their throats.

That had gotten Michael's curiosity up. He crept down the stairs as quietly as he could, avoiding the creaky third board from the top. He made it about halfway down, then sat on the steps and poked his head around the corner to peer through the railing. The basement was dark and lit only by a few tall candles his mother had set in high stands in the corners of the room.

Michael's mother and sister had their backs to the staircase and were wearing what looked like black silk robes. His mother was gesturing with a long knife, the blade already covered in blood that dripped down onto her hand. Both women were still chanting in unison in whatever the foreign language was. Their heads were thrown back, their eyes shut. And they were standing in front of Michael's father, who was lying down on a table in the center of the room.

Michael's father's eyes were open wide, mostly unfocused but with an edge of fear in them, and his mouth was working but no sounds were coming out. His chest was bare, and some kind of weird symbols were carved lightly into his skin. They were still bleeding but Michael could make out what looked like some kind of Satanic symbol. His father's arms and legs were lashed down with leather straps. His body was completely still; only his lips were moving. Michael froze, paralyzed with indecision, terrified and unable to cry out and ask his mother and sister what they were doing to his father.

His father had never been the perfect dad, but he wasn't a bad guy. He just liked his sports and beer and hanging out with his buddies a hell of a lot more than he liked staying home and being a husband and a father to two kids constantly screaming for his attention. Michael learned not to bother his father when he was watching a game, and to get him a beer when he asked for one, and not to get too bad of grades in school. Crossing his father meant a whipping with his belt. And his father was a strong man with a heavy hand, who had no qualms about using that belt. He even spanked Angela—*hard*—when she got into too much trouble. For all that, growing up, Michael had always loved his father, even though theirs was a distant relationship.

But all that had changed about five years prior, when Michael was thirteen. His parents had never gotten along well, but their arguments had been growing increasingly worse as life and the marriage moved on, with ever more frequent shouting matches and broken dishes. It had all come to a head late one night. Michael awoke to hear his parents downstairs, yelling even worse than usual. His father hadn't come home after work, but had apparently gone out drinking. When he finally arrived home—drunk—Michael's mother started hectoring him in her shrill voice. He began cursing her, calling her a filthy *strega* and telling her that all their money problems were caused by her superstition and obsession with spells and witchcraft rather than going out and getting a job. The argument escalated and Michael heard glass breaking. His mother was getting worked into even more of a frenzy than she usually did, when he heard a sharp crack and thud. Then complete silence. A few minutes later, he heard his father clomping up the stairs, heading into their bedroom, and slamming the door. Eventually he heard his mother crying downstairs, then she slammed the front door and left.

The next day, Michael's mother sent him over to spend the night with a friend. When Michael returned home the day after, Michael knew that something had changed between his parents; *something* had happened to his father. He wasn't the same man he was when Michael had last seen him.

Michael's father was a broken man after that. All the life had been drained out of him. He would come home from work every night and begin doing all the work around the house that his wife had left for him. No more drinking, no more football games, no more yelling or arguments. He simply dragged himself along from one task to another, never talking unless asked a direct question, and then he would only respond briefly in a quiet monotone. He never looked Michael, or anyone else, in the eye again. When he was done with the list of chores for the night, he would make himself a sandwich, wolf it down while standing in the kitchen, then head to bed for the night, not emerging until it was time for him to get ready for work the next day. Michael sometimes noticed his mother watching smugly with her arms crossed as his father did the chores she had ordered him to do. Michael asked his mother not long after what had changed in his father.

"Michael, your father learned that he should never have crossed me, and he learned that he should never, ever hit a woman. Especially a *strega*." She laughed and walked away. Michael never inquired further, and he always tried to give his mother a wide berth after that. Sure, she was crazy, but why take chances?

It was around that same time that Michael's sister Angela became much closer with their mother. His mother and Angela would often spend hours down in the basement together. They made it abundantly clear that Michael and his father were never to go down there unless specifically ordered to.

Angela started bossing their father around soon after, just like their mother did. Where previously their father would have slapped Angela or sent her to her room without dinner for talking to him that way and ordering him around, he now just silently accepted her orders, doing whatever she told him to. That made Michael feel worse than anything.

Michael also started to notice that once his father had changed—in whatever way he had—that his mother's interest in magic and witchcraft seemed to increase. He and his father had always shared a skepticism for what his father called "superstition from the Old Country." She now seemed to spend much of her time involved in reading about and studying witchcraft. Michael's sister Angela also seemed to start taking a real interest in it as well, which their mother encouraged. Family life soured, and Michael became more and more isolated from his family, withdrawing as much as he could and still live under the same roof. That was years before, and things had only deteriorated over time.

Michael snapped himself out of his reverie. His mother and sister's chanting, still incomprehensible to Michael, was picking up speed, almost becoming feverish in intensity. Michael watched from his vantage point on the steps, trying to figure out what was going on. Their chanting reached a climax, then stopped abruptly. Without hesitation, his mother raised her right hand, the one holding the knife. His gaze was rapt. He wanted to do something, say something, stop what was going on but he couldn't. Michael opened his mouth, but no sound came out.

The world seemed to stop for an instant. The blade of the knife paused in mid-air, above her head, and caught the candles' light, glinting.

The knife plunged down, all the way to the hilt, in the center of his father's chest, directly inside the symbol she had scratched there. His father exhaled a long sigh, his lungs and chest seeming to deflate. His eyes bugged out, then he went still.

Michael found himself suddenly able to move. He half stood, half crouched and threw himself over the railing and onto his mother's back. He caught her high up on her back, grabbing a hold of her hair and robe. She fell forward, across Michael's father, and the blood-covered dagger went flying out of her grip. She wasn't a large woman, but she was strong and quick, and she immediately began yelling and flailing her arms. She managed to push him backwards off of her, and he lost his grip, falling to the floor. His sister immediately got into the act and began scratching and tearing at his face. Michael pushed Angela away from him, and she stumbled backwards. He got a quick glimpse of his sister hitting against the wall, her head striking it hard. He saw her start to slide down the wall, her eyes closed, and then his mother was on top of him.

Michael's mother had managed to retrieve the knife, and she brutally tried to plunge it into his chest. He was amazed at how frenzied she was—the woman who had given birth to him and who, theoretically at least, was supposed to love him. Her eyes were wild, crazy, animalistic. Michael knew she would kill him here in the basement, just like she had killed his father. He got a deep scratch along his forearm as he deflected the blow meant to disembowel him. He grabbed his mother's wrist and twisted it back, forcing her to let go of the knife. It fell to the floor, and he kicked it away, out of both their reaches. Michael backhanded his mother as hard as he could, then he grabbed her arms and pushed her again. She fell against a table in the corner supporting a handful of long taper candles. The tables and candles both fell over, igniting the sleeve of her robe and the ratty old carpeting covering the basement floor, as the lit candles rolled everywhere. She started screaming, batting at her sleeve but only succeeding in spreading the flames further across her body. Her robe seemed to burn with unnatural speed. She started running around the room, her movements jerky and increasingly frantic. She accidentally toppled a tall bookcase, trapping herself underneath it. The bookcase and the books that spilled out of it began to smolder on the carpet, the flames starting to lick at them around the edges.

Michael stood there panting for several minutes, just watching.

The scene was surreal, dreamlike, nightmarish. He couldn't believe that any of this was really happening, had already happened. He watched his mother on her hands and knees, almost completely engulfed in fire by now, drag herself out from under the bookcase. Her robes and hair were covered in flames. She wasn't even trying to put them out anymore, she was just kneeling there with her head thrown back. A thin keening was coming from deep within her lungs. His sister was slumped down on the carpet against the wall, her head resting on her chest. Little flames were starting to dance around her feet. Michael looked over at his father, laid out on the table. His chest was now completely covered in blood, as was the table and the carpet around the table.

The fire was creeping up the walls of the basement. The paint on the walls was starting to blacken and blister. The entire carpet was completely ablaze, and now so were some old boxes in the corner. The room was starting to fill with oily black smoke that burned his eyes and made him want to cough and breathe fresh air more than anything else.

Michael knew that he had to leave now, or he'd soon be dead with the rest of the family. No way he could put the fire out at this point. He briefly thought about all of his stuff that was about to be destroyed. It was the books that pained him the most. He had scrimped and saved, done countless odd jobs, to buy them one by one, and had built up a pretty nice collection. He had almost complete runs of everything from the mysteries he had read as a kid—*The Hardy Boys*, *Encyclopedia Brown*, and *The Three Investigators*—to the fantasy (Tolkien and LeGuin), science fiction (Herbert and Niven), and horror (Lovecraft and King) he had gotten into the last couple years. Screw it. They were just books. Certainly nothing worth dying for. Michael ran up the stairs and out of the house as fast as he could. He knew the whole place was going to catch fire. He never looked back. He didn't bother to grab any of his stuff—all he had was his wallet and a small knife in his front pocket—he just kept running. He ran all the way over to an older buddy's house and stayed with him for a few days, then went out on his own after he caught wind that DC's finest were starting to nose around and ask questions about him. They never tried very hard to find him, and eventually the case was closed as a murder-suicide.

#

I hadn't seen Angela in thirteen years since that afternoon. To be honest, I didn't even care if she got out of the house alive. She was up to her eyeballs in whatever that foul ritual was my mother had cooked up. She certainly seemed like a willing participant to me. Fuck her. I always hoped she was rotting in hell like my mother. I hadn't thought about Angela in years. What a hell of a way for her to show up back in my life. She must have been brooding about me taking her mother away from her for all these years, and Jack was just payback for it. Revenge really *is* a dish best served cold, I guess.

CHAPTER 12

I stood there stunned for a few seconds while they all drove off. Jack was still half-kneeling there at the top of the stairs, blood just pouring out of him and pooling on the first couple steps. I couldn't tear my eyes away. He crumpled to the ground, face first, his arms hanging down the stairs. I ran over to him, tried to turn him over, but he was heavy and dead weight. Not dead though, please, God. I got him turned over and knew there was nothing I could do. He looked up at me and tried to say something, but nothing came out except that wheezing. I watched the light go out of his eyes. I sat there cradling him for a long time. I should have killed my sister when I killed our mother. Why the fuck hadn't I killed that bitch when I had the chance? None of this would have happened if I had just had the balls to kill her back them. Stab her, push her into the fire, whatever. Anything! Anything to prevent this from happening.

"Goddamnit!" I shouted at no one at all. A couple people had come over by now, but they didn't look terribly inclined to get involved with some guy kneeling with a bloody mess cradled in his arms.

I knew only one thing: I was going to make my sister pay for killing Jack. He was the closest thing I ever had to a real father, and she took him away—just like our mother killed our father. Yeah, I still wanted to get Fat Man and Little Boy, because if it hadn't been for them, none of this would have happened. But I knew my sister was really the one to blame. I'm sure it was her idea to grab Jack and use him as leverage against me. She had probably been stalking me for a long time, learning whatever she could. Dammit, I wish I had taken the time to make sure she had really died in that fire at some point in the last thirteen years. Maybe we could have worked it out somehow. Jesus, she didn't have to kill Jack. Crying would be very easy right now, and I can't even remember the last time I cried. Maybe when Jenny dumped me. God, get rid of *that* train of thought. Gotta stay focused, gotta stay in the game. I forced myself to get calm through sheer willpower. Hard to say how long that was going to hold.

I hated to do it, but I was going to have to leave Jack here. I didn't want to just leave him here in the care of strangers, but there was no way I was going to get wrapped up as his killer by the none-too-competent DC homicide squad. If I was being sweated in an interrogation room at the local police station, there was no way I'd ever be able to catch his killers and stop whatever they had planned for the book.

As I was lifting Jack up and laying him down carefully, trying my best not to get covered with any more of his blood, his shirt came open a little, and his favorite "good luck charm" popped out. It was a small brown leather bag sealed tightly and filled with something that had always smelled really weird. I couldn't describe the scent if you had a gun to my head. Jack had always claimed he got it from some New Orleans voodoo queen he was fucking back in the seventies. He swore that it was proof against harmful magics and would always keep him safe. He had offered to get one for me, but I always had my doubts. There was just something about it. Some little voice in the back of my head that told me Jack would have wanted me to take it. I gently eased it from around his neck and put it on under my shirt. I told myself I was taking it as much as a memento of Jack as anything else.

I eased him down and starting walking back down the blood-slicked Exorcist Stairs. I heard one of the passers-by say "Hey!" half-heartedly, but no one tried to stop me. I piled back in my car and tore out. Now I needed the Bookworm's help.

CHAPTER 13

The Bookworm's front door was hanging off its hinges when I got there. Not a good sign. It was a miracle that one of the neighbors hadn't seen or heard the commotion and called 911. The police actually respond to emergency calls in Glover Park, unlike most of the rest of the District. I pushed past the door and entered the vestibule. Peered into the living room. The place was a mess, with papers everywhere, an endtable knocked over, and a bookcase on the floor leaking books. Books were sprawled all over the floor, some with spines cracked or pages bent. It was a horrifying sight for any bibliophile. The Bookworm was *not* going to be happy about this. I walked slowly back through his house, heading toward his library and office, trying not to step on anything or make a sound. Whoever did this might still be around—I was assuming that Fat Man, Little Boy, and my sister had come by here before our little rendezvous, but I couldn't be sure and didn't feel like taking my chances. No way they could have beaten me here after they killed Jack and done all this. I really didn't want to tangle with anyone who could invade the Bookworm's home turf and wreak this kind of havoc.

I passed through the living room and kitchen, surveying the damage, then headed down the hallway to his library. The library door was open, so I poked my head around the doorframe cautiously and looked inside. The Lector was kneeling on the floor by the Bookworm, who was flat on his back, moaning quietly. Looked like he was beaten up pretty badly, but he was still moving around. For a second, the Lector moved aside, and I noticed the worst of it: the Bookworm's eyes were bloody red pits.

"Jesus!" I said involuntarily.

The Lector spun around, faster than I could have imagined, coming up into a kind of half-crouch. There was a kind of sparkly, neon green light surrounding her hands. That didn't look good.

"It's OK, it's just me! It's me, Augustino!" I stepped out into the doorway and held my hands out so she could see them.

Her face lost the tenseness and anger, almost crumbling. The light surrounding her hands winked out and tears welled up in her eyes. "Oh, Augustino, they—"

"It's OK, it's OK . . . ." I pulled her into an embrace and hugged her tightly. She didn't seem to be hurt too badly though. The Lector's eyes were red, her cheeks tear-stained and bruised. She also had one of the biggest knots on the side of her head I've ever seen.

"Jesus, that must have hurt," I observed astutely.

She nodded and said quietly, "It was Fat Man and Little Boy who did all this. They were with a woman, I don't know who she was. I've never seen or heard of her before. The worst part was, they didn't even think me worthy to consume my power. They just knocked me out, tied up my hands, then went to work on the Bookworm. When I woke up, they had already eaten . . . ." She started crying.

I put my arms around her and tried to comfort her the best I could, but after all she had been through, I'm not sure it meant much. The Lector seemed like she was running on auto-pilot anyway. Eventually she said, "That woman they were with was just as foul as they were, I could sense it. Evil was coming off her in waves."

"Yeah, I know. She's my sister."

The Lector gave me a look. I could tell she wasn't sure whether or not to believe me.

"It's true, I grew up with that bitch, but I haven't seen her since she was sixteen. Sure turned out great, didn't she? Just like our mother." I was babbling.

"Should we, um, should we call the cops, or take him to the hospital or something? We can put him in my car, and I can take him to Georgetown, I'm sure they could help...."

She cut me off right away. "No. No hospitals. I already tried to suggest that to him, but he didn't want to do that. He doesn't want to involve the police or doctors or anything like that. It would bring too much attention to him, to his house. He'd never be able to operate here in DC again. We'd have to move. They might arrest us. I don't know what exactly would happen." She looked up, directly in my eyes. "Just promise me, Augustino. You won't bring the authorities into this."

I promised her. I thought it was probably a lousy idea. I knew damn well he needed to see a doctor. Hell, he probably needed to be checked into an Intensive Care Unit. He'd had his eyes pulled out of his head for God's sake. But I also knew that as soon as the emergency room took one look at him, they'd call the police, and even DC's finest could figure out where he lived. They'd send detectives around to check out his house, no matter what story he could come up with.

"I need you to promise me something else, Augustino." I nodded for her to go on. "I need you to promise me that you'll help me get revenge on them for what they've done to him. I couldn't live with myself if I just let them go after what they've done, what they've taken away from him. I don't think they had the book yet though, because they were trying to get him to tell them where it was, and then they rampaged through the house looking for it, so it's not too late. We can still stop them. They have at least some measure of the Bookworm's power now, I don't know how much because I don't really understand how their magic works. At least they don't have the book, so they can't begin the ritual."

I really didn't want to tell her what had happened, for all kinds of reasons. She had to know what had happened though. It took me a long time before I could the words out. "Lector . . . they . . . they do have the book. I was able to get my hands on the book late last night. They kidnapped my partner Jack and offered to trade the book for Jack. I just came from there. They killed Jack anyway, even though I gave them the book." I couldn't look the Lector in the eyes. "My sister—my own fucking sister—cut his throat right in front of me, in broad daylight in Georgetown! I left Jack's body there on the sidewalk, and I came right here."

"I swear to you, though, I *will* avenge both Jack and the Bookworm. There's no way I could ever let this go, not after what they've done today. And you're right, with the Bookworm's power and the book, they're extremely dangerous. Even more so than they were."

I heard the Bookworm moan softly behind her. We both turned to him, crouched down beside him. I could tell the Bookworm was either in shock, or close to it. Hell, I found it amazing that he wasn't comatose or dead. Not everyone can be even marginally coherent an hour or two after they have their eyes ripped out of their skull.

He licked his lips. It took him a couple tries, but he eventually got out "Augustino?" in a soft voice.

"Right here, Bookworm. I'm right here. It's me—Augustino. You look like hell but you're going to be all right though." I put my hand on my shoulder. Like anything I could say or do at this point would matter.

"Augustino . . . it was the Fat Man. He was here with Little Boy and a woman I didn't know. He doesn't have the book yet, Augustino. There's still time."

I hated to be the bearer of even worse tidings to a man who had just had his eyes ripped out, but the Bookworm had to know. I gave him the quickie version of my life for the last day and a half.

"Then it's even worse than I had thought."

His words damned me. I basically *knew* it had been a trap when I went to meet them. I thought I could handle it. I thought I could take care of the whole thing. I thought I could trade the book for Jack, then Jack and I could show how smart we were and get the book back before any harm could be done.

I was wrong. So, so wrong. And Jack had paid the price for my failure and stupidity. The Bookworm had paid a pretty steep price too.

"I know, Bookworm, I know. Look, all hope isn't lost though. I can still get the book back. The ritual takes time, right? I flipped through the book when I still had it, and it looked complicated as hell. Someone who wanted to enact the ritual would have to study it for a while right? Prepare for it? Don't you wizards always have to gather rare materials, eye of newt, a virgin's blood, and all that shit? And wait for the right phase of the moon or something?" I was grasping at straws at this point. I had no idea where to find the Fat Man and my sister. I was going to have to start that search from scratch. Shouldn't be impossible to find out where he lived, though. Someone around town had to know, didn't they?

"Yes, it will take some time for them to study the ritual. But with all three of them working on it, it shouldn't take them *too* long. They could probably be ready to cast it tonight, if all goes well for them. While I haven't read the entire ritual, I have seen it referenced in several other texts. None mention any particularly rare materials or physical objects required. Nor have I seen any mention of a special timeframe in which the ritual must be completed. I assume that Tiamat wanted to make it as easy as possible for someone to contact it. I don't suppose you made a photocopy of the book, or at least the ritual?"

Dammit, one more thing I probably should have thought of. All I can say is, that message from the Fat Man and Jack threw me for a loop. I clearly hadn't been thinking straight. I shook my head no in response to his question, then after a couple seconds realized he couldn't see me, so I verbalized my answer. Jesus, I had lost a partner today, but the Bookworm had lost his *eyes*. And had them eaten right in front of him. I hoped he had passed out before that happened.

The Bookworm wasn't looking so good. I figured he needed to just rest a bit if we weren't going to be getting him to a doctor anytime soon. I helped the Lector bandage the Bookworm's eyes as best we could and get him muscled into a sitting position in his desk chair. I went and got him some water from the kitchen, along with an afghan to cover him up a bit. The Lector and I let him rest there and went into the hallway to talk quietly.

"He seems to be holding up a lot better than I would have imagined, given the circumstances," I told her. "Still, though, I think we need his help in tracking down the book. Is there anything you can do to help him out? Magically, I mean?"

"What do you think I've been trying to do for the last hour? I was able to help him some, give him a little energy boost, stabilize his system some, get the bleeding stopped, that sort of thing. But healing magic isn't my specialty. That's a very esoteric area of magic, one not many practitioners are able to delve into. It takes just the right kind of person, the right frame of mind. Plus, it can be very difficult, very dangerous, for both the healer and the person being healed. I just don't know how to do much more for him than I've already done."

"OK, I understand. Really I do. It's just that he's probably the only one who really knows anything about the book. I mean, I guess

I could try to talk to the Lich, maybe see if I can convince him to help us . . . ."

She practically hissed at me. "No! The Lich? Are you out of your mind? There's no way we can involve him! He wants the book for himself. There's no way he'd let us keep the book, even if he did agree to help. He's almost as bad as the Fat Man, in his own way." I started to protest; the Lich has never struck me as being a particularly bad guy. Weird as all hell, but who isn't these days?

She could see I wasn't immediately agreeing with her, so she played her trump card. "He's dead for God's sake!"

Some days I'm a little slow on the uptake. "He's dead? I just spoke with him last night. He was perfectly fine, at least as fine as he ever is . . . ."

"Look, Augustino, do you know what the word "lich" means?"

I shook my head. "No, not veally. I figured it was just one of those crazy names you guys like to go by." I know more about magic than the average Joe on the street, but that's about it.

"A lich is a wizard who has achieved a kind of immortality. He removes his soul from his body, places it inside some physical object, then kills himself, while simultaneously casting a spell to bring himself back to life. It's insanely difficult. Most wizards who try it fail and just end up committing an elaborate form of suicide and lose their souls in the process. Besides, the ritual is pretty much unknown to modern practitioners. I have no idea where he found it. Even if the ritual succeeds, the wizard is changed forever. I mean, think about it: his soul has been ripped out of his body and put inside something else, and his mind is inhabiting a corpse. Forever. That's *got* to do something to a person's psyche."

It was starting to make a bit more sense now. It was a lot to take in, but it was starting to come together. "You know, he's not a bad guy, for a dead man."

The Lector gave me one of her patented disapproving looks. Damn, she was good at that, even with that knot on her forehead and all.

"OK, OK, I won't contact him for help. He's even creepier than I had thought he was. Besides, we probably shouldn't introduce any more players into the game at this point anyway. I say we let the Bookworm rest for a bit, then we start quizzing him on what he thinks we ought to do. I've gotta tell you, my batteries are pretty drained. I could use a break for a minute myself here. And I don't have a helluva lot of ideas on how we can track down the book right now. I'm hoping that you guys can give me some leads."

I could tell the Lector needed to sit down herself for a bit. Hell, she had been knocked unconscious an hour or two ago herself. We went into the kitchen, I sat down, and the Lector made some tea. I don't drink the stuff, but I cracked open a Miller Lite I found in their fridge. I gulped down the beer like it was water, then went back for another one while the Lector finished making her tea. We sat down at the kitchen table in companionable silence for a while and just tried to relax. As if that was going to be possible. Eventually, I pushed my chair back from the table and said, "OK, that's gotta be enough of a break for now. Let's go back and harass the Bookworm about what our next options are."

It was hard to tell if the Bookworm was awake or not when we re-entered his library. He wasn't moving, and his head was resting on his desk. He started when the Lector went over and gently touched his shoulder. She talked quietly to him for a minute or two. I couldn't make out exactly what she was saying to him. The Lector beckoned me over. "How're you doing, Bookworm?" I asked quietly, squatting down next to him.

"I hurt like hell, Augustino. Physically, mentally . . . I just hurt like hell. Augustino, you need to know that the Fat Man now has at least some of my magic. That, added to his own abilities makes him even more formidable. I don't know how much of my magic he'll be able to assimilate, but he's succeeded in weakening me, and potentially augmenting his own abilities. That and . . . I'm blinded for life now." His voice trailed off. "Oh God . . . I'll never read again . . . ." I couldn't watch the Bookworm cry bloody tears. It was just too much after what I had already been through. I walked out of the room and let the Lector comfort him. I walked back into the living room, uprighted a chair, and sat down to think. OK, I sat down to brood, but you know what I mean.

After a few minutes, the Lector came and got me. When I got back to the Bookworm's library, he looked like he had mostly gotten a hold of himself.

"I don't recognize your sister's magic, Augustino. She's definitely a sorceress of some sort, but I can't say that I've ever encountered any similar practitioners. It was dark, dark stuff, Michael. Some kind of blood magic."

"I can't say that I'm surprised you'd say that about her, Bookworm. I just watched her cut my partner's throat in cold blood. She didn't even have to, dammit. I had already given them the book. Our mother introduced her to magic when she was a teenager. It's some kind of old Sicilian blood and vendetta magic. She's taken after our mother even more than I knew. I watched them kill my father in some kind of black magic ritual." I actually felt a slight amount of relief in telling them that. Jack and Jenny, the woman who I had thought was the love of my life, were the only two people I had ever told. The Lector put her hand on my shoulder. I was surprised that such a simple gesture meant so much to me. "I thought she was dead all these years, Bookworm. If I had known she was still alive, I would have . . . ." Well, I'm not sure exactly what I would have done.

After a minute, the Bookworm continued. "Lector, you're going to have to try to scry for the location of the book. Right now, I'm worthless. I can't see, and I certainly can't cast the spell. I may not ever be able to cast another spell, I don't know yet. I know that the Fat Man took some, maybe all, of my magic when he devoured my eyes. You know what you need to do though, and I'll be here to render whatever assistance I can. I've trained you well, and you're a quick study. You'll be fine."

The Lector nodded. She left the room for a minute and came back with a stack of $100 bills. She took a pair of scissors and carefully cut out all the portraits of Benjamin Franklin. God, it killed me watching her do that. I couldn't help but wonder if a bank would exchange them for new bills. While she was doing that, the Bookworm told me where to find his big spiral-bound ADC map book of the entire DC metropolitan area. I spread it open on his desk.

I watched the Lector prepare herself. She sat across from the Bookworm at his desk, gazing intently at the map for a while, then closed her eyes and almost seemed to have entered into a Zen-like state when she opened them a minute later. Her gaze was piercing, fixed only on what she was doing. She carefully laid out thirteen cut-outs of Ben Franklin's head in a pattern surrounding the District's borders, then started mumbling or chanting under her breath. Her voice was too soft for me to catch anything that she was saying. Hell, I probably didn't speak whatever language she was using anyway—I skipped most of my ancient Lemurian classes.

Nothing happened for a while, then the little cut-out portraits spread out, all by themselves, flying and hovering around and around, just above the map. All of a sudden they seemed to shift their positions and stop in mid-air for a second, then fell. They had distributed themselves evenly, covering the entire District. Not an inch of the map was left uncovered.

The Lector seemed to snap out of her trance. She stared at the map.

"What the hell does *that* mean?" I wondered aloud.

"What? What?" The Bookworm obviously wanted to know what the outcome of the Lector's scrying attempt had been.

"Fuck. It failed. Same as last time." I had been expecting a more technical explanation from the Lector, but that would do just fine.

The Bookworm's face crumpled. I'm sure it was no worse than my own expression. Dammit! I had been banking on a magical solution to the problem. Which was stupid, of course; if I've learned one thing in my time working with Jack, it's that magic's never a solution, it's just one more problem.

I had no idea if the scrying had failed because the Lector just wasn't powerful enough to do it, or because of something the Fat Man had done to protect himself and the book from detection. I suspected the latter was the case. So did the Bookworm. "The spell should work under ordinary circumstances. The portraits of Benjamin Franklin should all have clustered on the spot where the book is. Since Franklin was the author of the book, that should have been a powerful enough tie to link the cut-out pictures with the book's location. But obviously the scrying is being blocked by a more powerful magic."

Well, clearly magic wasn't going to be helpful here. We were at somewhat of a loss. We still had to find the book, so that left guesswork. Hopefully educated guesswork. We brainstormed for a couple hours and ate a surprisingly good meal cooked by the Lector. She was certainly useful for more than just reading the Bookworm's books for him. She and I both looked up various esoteric points in reference texts at the Bookworm's insistence. There was a lot of mystic/esoteric bullshit theorizing, but the argument boiled down to this: the ritual had to be conducted in a world power center—Washington DC certainly fit that requirement just fine—so it made sense that the Fat Man and my sister would remain in town. Within the power center, the ritual had to be connected at either the highest point geographically or the lowest because those were the points where the mystical barriers or boundaries between our world and whatever hellhole Tiamat inhabited were thinnest.

As it turns out, the highest point in DC is the National Cathedral just south of Tenleytown in Upper Northwest. That was pretty specific, plus it's a significant location. Hell, it was included in L'Enfant's original plan for the city. Countless nationally important religious ceremonies had been held there over the years. The lowest point on the surface of the Earth in DC, though, is along the Potomac River shoreline. We knew that the location had to be significant in some way, and appropriate to the ritual. The National Cathedral worked because it was symbolically the focal point for the entirety of the most powerful nation on Earth to contact a higher being. We could see how that could be ritualistically linked to summoning Tiamat. The DC shoreline was a little harder to link symbolically. None of us could come up with any one location along the shoreline that would have specific ritual significance to opening a portal between our world and some kind of hell dimension. Then it hit me.

"Hains Point."

"What?" said the Bookworm.

"Hains Point. It's a little park wedged between the Jefferson Memorial and the 14th Street Bridge. Haven't you ever been there?"

"Not that I can recall. But why would it have any locational significance to the ritual?"

"Well, right at the far end of the park, surrounded by water on both sides is this really weird-ass sculpture. It's made of dark metal, and it's probably a hundred feet long. The parts that are above ground are the arms, legs, and head of a giant who looks: one, seriously pissed off, and two, like he's bursting up out of the ground. Doesn't that sound perfect to you? Some weird mythological creature waking up and bursting out of the ground? Sounds like the kind of place that would be right up Tiamat's alley. It's symbolic of some creature coming from one dimension into ours, see?"

The Bookworm and the Lector both liked the idea, especially the Lector. That made me feel better, she's one smart cookie, despite—or because of?—the fact that she usually won't say more than two sentences to me. (Except when her boss' eyes got ripped out, that is.)

Ultimately though, the Bookworm wouldn't budge. He was convinced they would be conducting the ritual inside or on the grounds of the National Cathedral, while I (and the Lector) were convinced they would be down at the shoreline, probably at the tip of Hains Point. We all figured they would be attempting to contact Tiamat as soon as possible, since we, and potentially other clued-in individuals and power-seekers, were onto them. Now I'm not an expert on magic, and I'm certainly no wizard, but my theory made perfect sense to me.

So naturally, I decided to head over to Hains Point first, then quickly head back to the cathedral if I was wrong. Besides, screw him, it was my ass on the line. God, was that ever a mistake.

Before I left though, I remembered someone who Jack had once introduced me to. I looked up his name and number, since the Lector and the Bookworm were still dead set on not taking him to the hospital. He was an old, disbarred alchie "doctor" who Jack had known for a long time. I had him in my little black notebook I carry with me everywhere; there were surprisingly few attractive women listed there and far too many old men and freaks. Such is my life. I had played cards with the doc a few times. He was an easy mark because he kept drinking and drinking vodka as the night went on, and his cardplay suffered commensurately. He never looked or smelled drunk in the least, though, which I found amazing. I would have been passed out on the floor and choking to death on my own vomit if I consumed as much liquor as he did during some friendly card games.

After that first card game, Jack had given me the guy's number in case I ever got shot or knifed or something; basically, if I got some kind of injury that would raise way too many uncomfortable questions at a hospital. Jack knew me too well. Fortunately for me, I had never been in desperate enough straits that I had had to call upon his services. I called him up now though, and he agreed to come over to the Bookworm's place and check him out. I hung up and hoped that he wasn't halfway into a daylong binge. I gave the Lector his number and told her to harass him every five minutes if he hadn't shown up within an hour. It was long after sundown by now, and I headed out to the car to see what, if anything, was happening at

Hains Point.

As I was leaving, the Lector came out onto the front porch with me. She stepped in close. "Look, Augustino, I just want you to know that I appreciate all you've done so far, and I can't tell you how sorry I am to hear about your partner. I guess none of us realized how vicious the Fat Man and your sister could be. What you're doing is incredibly important...and brave . . . and stupid. You've got to know that you're in way over your head, right?"

I nodded. "Somebody's got to go after them. Might as well be me, I guess." I followed that up with my patented smile—you remember the one—and for the first time ever, the Lector smiled back.

She reached into her blouse and pulled out an amulet of some kind: a silver chain and a small pendant thing with what looked like an opal in the middle. "I want you to take this with you," she said as she began unfastening it from around her neck. "This is my journeyman piece."

"Your what?"

"Well, the Bookworm comes from a fairly formal tradition of magical practitioners, and he's training me in that tradition. I'll tell you more about it some other time. We have more pressing issues to deal with right now than occult esoterica. Long story short, though, is that when I was ready to move from beyond a mere apprenticeship under the Bookworm to a journeyman position, I had to undergo a test. Thank God, you only have to do that once, assuming you succeed. Part of the test is the construction of a unique magical device, one that embodies part of yourself. Part of my essence went into that thing, so take care of it, will you?"

"What does it do?"

"Nothing to worry about. It may not do anything for you. It may help a little." I guess that's the best you can ask for when it comes to magic.

I leaned my head down a little, and she fastened it around my neck. I studied it for a few seconds, then put it under my shirt, along with the mojo bag I had gotten from Jack. "You put a piece of yourself into this thing? Really? Thanks. I think that's the sweetest gift I've ever gotten. I should give it back to you when I'm done then; I don't want to be responsible for losing it. I'll give it back to you after I have the book, how about that? Assuming I get the book back, of course . . . if not, I'll leave it to you in my will." She didn't smile at that.

"But what does it do, exactly?" I had to ask if I was going to be wearing this thing.

"Well, I'm not entirely sure what it will do for you. It would probably work a little differently for each person, depending on who's wearing it. It's fairly powerful, though, if I do say so myself. Even the Bookworm was impressed. He said it was better than his journeyman piece, and that's saying something. His was...well, I'll let him tell you about it himself some time. I'm giving this to you because I think that it just might serve as protection for you if someone is casting a curse or some other kind of malign spell on you. It's basically a warding or guardian piece. I guess I ended up putting some of my 'nuturing' side into it. I have to admit, though, I don't know exactly how it will work for you specifically. I can't make any guarantees. It probably wouldn't work against all kinds of harmful spells, though. Remember, it's not going to make you invincible, not even close to it. And, of course, you're still vulnerable to mundane attacks. You know, guns, knives, lead pipes to the back of the head. Pleasant things like that." I thanked her again.

"So what's the other thing I noticed you have around your neck?"

"What, this?" I said, taking out the little mojo bag thing I had taken off Jack after he died. Damn. I was starting to turn into a magic fetishist just like Jack. I already had two little magic gizmos around my neck. Next thing you know, I was going to start carrying around a pocket full of "lucky" trinkets just like Jack.

The Lector's reaction to the mojo bag surprised me a bit. She took a half step back and said, "Do you know what that thing *is*? Where did you get it?"

"Yeah, I got it from Jack. He was wearing it when he died. He always claimed he had gotten it as some kind of good luck charm down in New Orleans, years ago. I think it was supposed to be some kind of voodoo thing. For some reason, I took it off him and put it around my neck. Why? What is it? Is something wrong with it? I mean, it didn't exactly protect Jack from getting his throat slit." I was kind of alarmed by her reaction and started to pull it off.

"No, no, it's nothing bad," she said, putting her hand on mine to stop me from removing the bag. "I was just surprised, that's all. It's not anything that will hurt you. It may even help you some day.

Let's talk about it later, after all this is over. OK?" That was all right by me, so I put the bag back under my shirt.

Then the strangest thing in the last two days happened: the Lector leaned in, wrapped her hands around the back of my head, and gave me one of the best kisses I've ever had. I responded in kind, naturally. Wow, who knew? Not me, that's for sure.

I had no idea what to say, so after we finished the kiss, I smiled, waved, and walked out to my car. Not that she'd ever tell me, but I couldn't help but wonder what her real name was.

Heh. I'm a P.I. Maybe if I survive tonight, I'll try to figure that out.

CHAPTER 14

The gates to the park at Hains Point were closed off and locked at night, so I had to park nearby and walk in. No one but a mugger, a junkie, or an insane wizard would be out in the park at this time of night anyway. The tourists, joggers, and dog walkers had all long since headed home. I still wasn't quite sure if I had the right idea when I spotted a parked silver Ford Explorer right by the gate. Not that uncommon of a vehicle, but wasn't that what they were driving when they killed Jack in Georgetown?

I would have had to walk quite a ways to get to the end of the park where the statue was, so I decided to cover it in a light jog. Didn't want to waste time, but I also didn't want to be winded in case I was in for the fight of my life when I got to the statue.

There was quite a wind kicking up off the river, and I was glad I had my jacket on. My balls had shriveled up to the size of pecans, and I couldn't quite stop shivering. I made sure that my flipknife was still secure in my pants pocket and Jack's pistol was handy before I started my jog. I had moved the gun to my jacket pocket when I left the Bookworm's, because I was tired of having it press into the small of my back uncomfortably.

It took me longer to get to the end of Hains Point than I had expected, but then again, I'm not exactly the jogging type. I'm more of the get-in-the-car-and-go kind of guy. My idea of exercise usually involves watching other people exhaust themselves playing professional sports. I was feeling like an idiot and was a little out of breath by the time I got to the statue at tip of the peninsula. There was the statue all right, but no one was in sight. I figured the whole idea was probably a bust, but since I had come all this way, I might as well take a closer look around.

Nothing odd about the statue's legs—or at least nothing weirder than a pair of giant metal legs sticking out of the ground—and I still didn't see anyone. I was walking toward the head when I looked down to see what I had stepped in. Dog shit some good citizen hadn't bothered to clean up from earlier in the day. Great, just what I needed—

I heard a small scuffling sound, then something dark was flying through the air towards me from behind and to the side. Next thing I knew, I was falling forward, then was flipped flat on my back in the dirt in front of the giant's head.

It was Little Boy. He was kneeling on my chest, his hands on my throat and his weight pressing me into the dirt. It was a struggle just to breathe. The winter ground was frozen solid as a rock. "You know, Augustino" he said, putting his fat face in mine, "I'm going to eat you. Eat. You. Right. Up." He licked his lips and let out a giggle.

That was *not* what I wanted to hear right now.

"You're not my type, fatso." I pushed as hard as I could and gave him a heave. God damn he was heavy! He had his arms wrapped around me like a giant, hairy, smelly monkey. I was able to use a little leverage to push him to the side and get him off my chest a little, so at least I could take a deep breath again. "You need to go on the Atkins Plan."

I forced him over onto the ground, halfway on his side, and climbed on top of him as best I could, just as he had done to me. I planted a knee in what should have been his groin. His fat thighs seemed to absorb much of the blow, but he did give a satisfying wheeze. We rolled and tumbled around in the dirt for a while. Little Boy started to use his weight against me. He clearly wanted to get me underneath him so he could finish me off. I didn't like that idea, so I broke it off and got away from him, crab-crawling away until I was ten feet or so away. It took him a few seconds to stumble to his feet, which I used to try to catch my breath.

"You're not looking so good, fatty." I figured I might as well taunt him a bit, might get him mad enough to screw up. "Your face is all red, and I can hear you breathing all the way over here." Like I wasn't breathing hard myself.

"Shut up . . . just . . . shut the fuck up," he panted and wheezed.

Then Little Boy charged me, faster than I thought he could move, and though I caught his shoulders with both hands, he managed to force me back. I started sliding backward and couldn't get a good enough grip on either him or the frozen dirt. No traction and he was applying steady pressure on me. My heel caught on something and I fell backward. My head clanged into one of the statue's arms. It was blindingly painful and I saw stars. Honest-to-God stars. Always thought that was just in cartoons...I blacked out.

#

When I came to, I was sprawled out on the ground, my head and shoulders propped up against the statue's arm, apparently right where I fell. I had to blink a few times and rub my eyes to clear my head. When I opened them, I saw Little Boy standing about ten feet away. I didn't know what he was up to exactly; all I knew is that it looked magical and clearly didn't bode well for me.

Little Boy looked like he was starting to go into an epileptic seizure, he was waving his arms around so fast, in what I assumed he intended as mystic passes. His stubby little arms didn't have a terrific range of motion, but he was producing plenty of electric blue sparks. It was hard to make out. My vision was still a little blurry, but it looked like a weird, semi-transparent octopus-looking thing was forming in mid-air out of the blue electricity building up in front of him. Several of the tentacles looked like they were moving of their own accord. One of the tentacles started elongating, stretching out toward me, inching along in mid-air.

I tried to sit up, but couldn't seem to motivate myself to move off the statue. I was feeling so tired and lethargic, I could barely move my head. I just lay there watching Little Boy, fascinated by his movements for some reason. I felt woozy and light-headed, like I was a little drunk.

The blue electrical tentacle was now only about a foot away from my face, and even though that little voice in the back of my head was telling me to run, scream, fight, move, do something, anything, dammit!, I couldn't seem to motivate my body to obey. I lay there as the tentacle stopped a few inches away from my face, then darted toward me with blinding speed. I couldn't tell exactly what happened, but it looked like a little tiny pearly-pink bolt of lightning shot up from my chest and struck the tentacle, racing back along the tentacle toward Little Boy. What the hell *was* that lightning thing? Oh yeah, that had to be the Lector's handiwork, from her amulet. I clearly owed her a beer. More than one, actually. And maybe another kiss.

Little Boy let out a high-pitched yelp that would have been comical in other circumstances, and the entire electric blue octopus-thing collapsed and disappeared. I found that my body would now obey my brain, and I sprung up as fast as I could. I wasn't as quick as I might normally be, but I was faster than the surprised fatty.

I charged him and was in his face before he could really react. He looked shocked that I was even standing, and that his spell—or whatever that thing had been—had failed. I punched him, a glancing blow on his jaw, then bitch-slapped him, buffeting him around. I moved to his side and behind him, managing to get him twisted all the way around somehow. It wasn't easy; while Little Boy wasn't exactly the strongest guy on the planet, he certainly had mass on his side. I wrapped my right forearm around his throat and I held on as tightly as I could, squeezing his fat neck as hard as I possibly could. Little Boy didn't seem to like that one little bit. He started kicking and scratching and clawing at me, all in silence, since he couldn't make much more than a slight choking sound. Hell, he would have been gnawing at me with his teeth if I'd have let him. My arms were protected by my jacket, but my right hand was starting to get clawed up, and I could feel his spit and froth coating the forearm of my jacket. After a few more seconds, he started bucking hard trying to throw me off his back. Nothing doing. I knew this chokehold was my one shot to put him down. I finally managed to get my left hand up under my right elbow, which allowed me to really lay on the pressure.

It took a surprisingly long time—we're talking a couple minutes here, or at least it felt that way—but eventually Little Boy collapsed. Dropped to his knees, then fell face first into the dirt. I continued to squeeze

I'll admit it: I knew I was killing him. I knew it, and I didn't care. Not one bit. While he didn't personally kill Jack, he was there, so it was partly his fault. And he had already told me he was going to kill me here tonight. God only knows what that octopus thing he conjured up would have done to me. And trying his damnedest to off me just now didn't help matters.

He hadn't moved in a long while by this point, though I was still on top of him with my arms wrapped around his throat. Huh. Actually, I didn't feel bad about killing him at all. So that's what it feels like to kill someone: nothing. Nothing at all.

I had to sit down and think about that one for a minute or two. Sitting on that statue's arm, staring at Little Boy facedown in the dirt didn't make me feel bad at all. I had to think about what kind of person that made me.

Eventually, I decided that another time might be a better choice for psychoanalyzing myself and pondering what it means to kill a man, so I gave up on it, for now. I vaguely considered dumping Little Boy in the Potomac, but the water's edge was *awfully* far away, and he looked really friggin' heavy laying there. I left the fat bastard there and headed back to my car.

CHAPTER 15

Physically, I wasn't feeling so great. My head was throbbing, and I felt mildly nauseous. I rested a minute and jogged/limped back to the car as best I could. God, that was the longest jog of my life. Had to rest again in the car. Eventually, I pulled off into traffic, headed up to the National Cathedral. Now that I knew where Fat Man and my sister had to be, I was going to be better prepared. Dammit.

I assumed they didn't need Little Boy for the ritual so they had used him to bait a trap for me or whoever else might have come after them. He was probably a throw-away for them anyway, just there to take care of anyone who guessed incorrectly and buy them some time (at worst) or to get rid of the competition entirely (at best).

Now was not the time to get pulled over for a ticket, especially since the cops might be looking to question me about Jack's death, but I drove the absolute fastest I could, and then some. I pretended I was a Nigerian cabbie to get myself in the right frame of mind. I drove up Wisconsin Avenue to the National Cathedral and found a parking space on a side street. There was construction all along the front of the building, but the place was still open for business, at least during daylight hours. The cathedral grounds were completely dead. I walked around the building, not seeing anything amiss. I had half expected to see Fat Man and Streghina cavorting around a pentagram behind the cathedral. Not a damn soul in sight though.

I was looking for a way inside the cathedral when I made it around to the crypt entrance on the far side of the building. I was pretty sure that the side door wasn't supposed to be open this late at night, but it was slightly ajar and I slipped inside.

It was dark, quiet, and more than a little eerie inside. I guess crypts have a way of being like that. I knew that they were around here somewhere, and I *really* didn't want them jumping out from a darkened side chapel and ambushing me like Little Boy did. Of course, I also didn't want one of the cathedral's night watchmen to pull a gun on me and detain me until the cops arrived. I guess killing a man and getting away with it tends to make you a little paranoid.

As I was walking past one of the chapels on the crypt level, I spotted a pair of feet sticking out from under some chairs. I crept inside the chapel to take a closer look. It was a rent-a-cop lying flat on his back on the floor, asleep, unconscious, or dead. I got closer and crouched down beside him to check his pulse. Not that I needed to, really, his shirt was covered in blood and his throat was slit open. Jesus Christ. Well, that at least resolved the dilemma of if they were actually around here. The upside was that I had to assume that they would have already taken care of whatever security measures the cathedral had in place.

It took me a few minutes to check out the entire crypt level. The gift shop looked like it was still locked up tight, and other than that dead security guard, I hadn't seen anything suspicious to indicate that they were around here anywhere. I decided to head upstairs to the main body of the cathedral.

Jesus, this place was huge! No wonder they had so many important funerals here. You could squeeze thousands of people in here at once. No sign of a deranged wizard or my bitch of a sister though. The main body of the cathedral was completely dark and silent as a tomb. Not a creature was stirring, not even a mouse. I was wary though, because I knew they had to be here somewhere—that night watchman didn't coincidentally decide to cut his own throat.

The National Cathedral is laid out with two big towers in the front of the church, on either side of the front doors. There's an even taller tower located right above the center of the cathedral. I had taken the tour once, years ago, on a lark, but they didn't take us up the central tower at all, so I had no idea what is was like up there. I had been in the two smaller front towers, but they just had some meeting rooms, offices, small auditoriums, things like that. A great view of DC, but that was about it. I checked out the elevators to both the front towers, but they were both locked up and sitting on the first floor with me. I suppose Fat Man and my sister could have swiped the elevator keys from the security guard they whacked, then sent the elevator car back down once they arrived at the top, but somehow I doubted it. Besides, the two front towers were pipsqueaks compared with the big central tower. That *had* to be where they were. The top level or roof of that central tower literally would be the highest spot in all of Washington.

Just one problem though: where the hell were the elevators or stairs to the central tower? I ran back from the vestibule into the main body of the cathedral. I was almost frantic at this point; I knew they were around here somewhere, probably right up at the top of the central tower, but I couldn't find a way to get to them. Nothing immediately obvious anyway. After running around a bit, I spotted a staircase tucked away behind a door on the left side that I thought might take me up to a balcony or upper platform area. Who knew? Maybe there would be another staircase or elevator up there, leading to the central tower.

Whoever designed this place sure didn't want people to see how to get up to the top of the main tower. I knew it had to be possible, because that's where the bells are. There had to be a way to get up there to ring them and perform maintenance on them. I dashed up the staircase, which took me to a balcony area overlooking the main part of the cathedral. I was hoping I might spot something amiss from my new vantage point. Still nothing. They *had* to be up in the bell tower; I could see the entire inside of the cathedral from this vantage point.

Near the back of the balcony, there was a doorway to what turned out to be a very narrow spiral staircase heading straight up. This had to be it. I can't tell you how much fun it is to climb up an unfamiliar spiral staircase in pitch darkness, not knowing if two murderous sorcerers are going to pounce on you at any moment. Needless to say, I drew Jack's gun. I have to admit, that did make me feel a little better. I figured I could shoot anything that came down at me. I sure wouldn't want to get in a fight on these stairs though. Falling down these stairs would be a real bitch.

Oddly enough, my walk up the spiral staircase was uneventful. Tense and tiring, but uneventful. I made it up through the trapdoor to the roof and poked my head out. I immediately knew that Fat

Man and my sister were somewhere around. All the hairs on my head started trying to stand up. My skin felt prickly, like there were little tiny spiders or mites crawling all over me. I fought the urge to start scratching like crazy. Yep, there they were around here somewhere and working magic, from the creeped-out sensation I was getting.

The trapdoor let me out into an area of the roof that was off to one side and behind some kind of bulky machinery. No idea what those big metal boxes were—maybe something connected to the bell system, or more likely the cathedral HVAC system. There was a short railing, just a few feet high around the edge of the roof. Damn, I sure didn't want to take a long fall over the edge.

It was a moonless night, and most of the stars were obscured by cloud cover, so the roof was pitch black, except for a couple small twinkling lights on the other side of the machinery. I crouched down and peered over. Yep, there they were. Looked like the Fat Man and my sister had set up shop here. There was the usual assortment of mystical paraphernalia, including several candles—the source of the twinkling I had seen—in glass candle holders protecting them against the wind. The wind had definitely picked up since I was down at Hains Point, so I could see why they'd brought those. It was freezing up here, now that I thought about it, and wondered if I should have brought a heavier coat. Well, too late to worry about that now; and besides, a thicker coat would only have inhibited my movement.

Their backs were toward me, and they were intent on whatever it was they were doing. Streghina was chanting and cradling the book in her arms, while the Fat Man fiddled with something on the ground. Looked like he was doing something with a little hibachi. I wondered if I should just shoot them both in the back right now. That would be poetic justice, wouldn't it? I took aim at them—mentally debating which one I would shoot first—and tried to squeeze the trigger, but my finger just wouldn't do it. I'm a big pussy, I guess. I just couldn't do it. Damn, that would have been a perfect ending to a couple of rough days.

I decided to just waltz up to them instead. Gun at the ready, of course. I'm stupid, but I'm not that stupid. I walked around the machinery and said, "So, guys, how's it going?"

They both spun around. The look on the Fat Man's face was almost worth all the trouble I had gone through to get here. My sister merely broke off in mid-chant and eloquently asked, "What the fuck are you doing here?"

"I was in the neighborhood already, and since we're such great friends, I figured I'd stop by, see how you were doing, and oh, I don't know, maybe stop you from summoning Tiamat and reshaping the world in your own twisted images. How's that for starters?"

The Fat Man recovered quickly and simpered, "My, Augustino, you look like you've had a rough night."

"We can't all look as good as you, Fat Man."

"So how'd you get so roughed up, Augustino? Did you choose poorly and encounter our friend, Little Boy? He was most anxious to meet you this evening. I have to admit, I didn't give you enough credit. I didn't believe you'd actually be able to figure out where we'd be, or even if you did, I didn't think you'd have the balls to come looking for us. Not after seeing your partner die. Oh and has the Bookworm seen you lately? Ha ha! Oh, that's right, he can't! They were tasty, by the way...." The Fat Man chortled, then let out a dainty burp and covered his mouth. "Pardon me."

I came damn close to pulling the trigger.

"Shut up! Just shut the fuck up both of you!" my sister snapped. We both obliged. She had a way about her, I must admit. "We're not here to have some witty repartee and a tea party. A word to the wise: walk away, Michael. Just walk away. You don't have to die here tonight, like your partner. You have a choice: you can walk back down the steps, get in your car, and forget you ever saw us. Or you can die here on the roof tonight. Your choice. For all your faults, you were never stupid. Don't be stupid tonight. You truly don't understand the forces you're fucking with here."

"Aren't you forgetting one thing though, sis?"

"Like?"

"Like the gun I'm pointing at your sorry asses?"

The Fat Man made a sweeping arm gesture, leaving a trail of thin blue sparks in the air. Immediately it felt like sharp little claws were prying and scraping at my right hand—the hand holding Jack's gun. The pain was excruciating. I squeezed off a shot, but my aim was thrown off by the pain of invisible talons, or whatever the hell they were, and the shot went wild. The sound of it was loud in my ears, but the night wind swept it away. I doubted anyone in the city below would have even heard it. I held out a second longer, then the gun was wrenched out of my grasp, and went flying over the side of the cathedral, down onto the ground a hundred fifty feet away. Shit. That gun was the one advantage I had over these freaks.

"OK, I guess you guys hadn't forgotten about that. My bad."

"We don't have time to deal with your crap right now, Michael," my sister said. "We're at a delicate point in the ritual. We need to press on, or it will all be lost. I'm not starting over, so sit down over there and shut up while we finish."

I obliged by sitting down on the rooftop, my arms curled around my knees, trying to buy some time while I figured out what to do. I knew I could probably fuck up the ritual at least a little by kicking over the candles and stuff, but I also knew that it would cost me my life. I wasn't quite ready to do that. Not yet anyway. Nothing more I could do about it—for now.

The Fat Man gave me a dirty look, sniffed, and turned away to continue the ritual. He and my sister began chanting again, making the occasional gesture or throwing something smelly onto the hibachi and causing the flames to flare up. They took turns looking over at me to make sure I was staying put.

I knew that this was my one last shot to stop them from finishing the ritual. No way I was going to let them finish the ritual—they'd cut my throat just like they had with Jack to eliminate a loose end. Besides, I suspected that Tiamat might even be a little hungry when it got here, and I had no intention of being a midnight snack for either it or the Fat Man. If they succeeded in summoning Tiamat, I knew I was a dead man. Definitely not how I planned on ending things. Being desperate can sure make you do some crazy things, I guess.

So that was why I waited until what looked like a difficult part of the ritual absorbed both their attention, then sprung at the Fat Man's back, catching him around the waist and bowling him over, headfirst into the hibachi. He started screaming immediately. Probably because one cheek was being pressed into the grill. I would have been screaming like a little girl too, I have to admit. I couldn't hold him down long enough for my liking though. His flailing about quickly overturned the small grill, then we were rolling across the rooftop.

I was able to get in several very satisfying piledriver punches into the Fat Man's prodigious gut. My fists seemed to sink in halfway up to the elbow. It took the wind out of him for a second, then his cheeks inflated and turned purple, like a crazed Dizzy Gillespie. He seemed to muster all his strength then, because he was able to push me back—*hard*. I staggered back five or six feet, tripped over my own two feet or something on the roof, then fell onto my back, hitting my head pretty damn hard. I lay there for a second, just fighting to stay conscious. Shit. Raising my head a foot off the ground, even using both hands, was about all I could manage right now. Must have smacked my head harder than I thought. There was blood on my hand when I pressed it against the back of my skull. I hate when that happens.

I thought for sure I was toast. The Fat Man slowly walked over to me, standing right over my mostly prone body. He opened his mouth as wide as was humanly possible, maybe even a little more, then he spat some kind of energy ball at me, which looked like a blob of lava spitting black electrical sparks. The smell of it—like some kind of bile made out of pure evil—made me nauseous. It was fouler than anything I had ever smelled before (and that's saying something, given some of the kitchens I've worked in). Just before the blob struck me in the face, it veered toward my chest. I looked down and noticed that the Lector's pendant wasn't tucked inside my shirt any longer, but was sitting right there on top of my shirt. The pendant shone slightly, and the energy blob seemed to pause in mid-air. The blob was slowly sucked inside the opal in the center of the pendant, like some kind of viscous oil getting sucked down the drain. As the opal consumed the blob, it grew darker and darker. When the blob had disappeared entirely, the pendant's light faded away altogether. Shit. I think I broke the Lector's pendant. Still, that sucker had saved my life twice now. I guess I owed the Lector another beer. And a replacement pendant. That was going to be tougher to find.

The Fat Man looked like his magic loogie had worn him out. He was standing there incredulous and panting, trying to catch his breath. I figured it was now or never. I scrambled up, trying my damnedest to get to my feet, but I was still pretty shaky. I was trying desperately to get some kind of advantage, *something* I could use against the Fat Man, then I remembered my knife. Other than a tired Velcro wallet, that was the only thing I had to my name when I ran away from my burning home as a teenager. I pulled it out, flicked it open, and dove in for the kill. I managed to stab the blade into his abdomen almost to the hilt. It sank in like a hot knife cutting through butter, and I ripped it across his belly in an arc close to two feet long. I pulled out the knife and took a step back. He and I seemed to be equally amazed at what I had just done. I've never actually stabbed someone before, and I doubt the Fat Man had ever been stabbed. It was surprisingly easy; his belly was a little rubbery, but provided a shockingly small amount of resistance to the blade.

He had a dazed look on his face—what Jack always liked to call the "stunned mullet look"—as he stared down at his stomach. Blood was welling forth, just oozing out through the long rent in his shirt and belly. The Fat Man looked up at me, our eyes met, then he opened his mouth and more blood just poured down the front of his shirt.

Without saying a word, the Fat Man turned away and started trundling off, moving as fast as his bulk and injury allowed, heading for the trapdoor that led below. I could see that his meathooks were pressed tightly into his gut holding ropes of intestines inside. He was one tough bastard. I'd say anyone else would be a goner with that kind of injury, but I gave him a fifty-fifty shot of making it out of the cathedral alive. If he lived, I'd have to catch up with him and make sure he didn't. But right now I had bigger fish to fry, or at least one tough little Sicilian bitch.

"Not bad, Michael. Not bad at all. You're better than I had given you credit for. But I think you'll find I'm a little tougher than that fat fuck."

All of a sudden she was on my back, and I felt a blinding pain in my right ear, along with a sharp pulling sensation. Jesus, she was biting the shit out of my ear and was grinding through it with her teeth. It took me a second, but I was able to get my elbow up and gave her a crack right between the tits then another one in the mouth. She released my ear—I think it was still attached, it felt like it was on fire—and I pushed myself back and away from her. I reached up to touch my ear. Fuck! It was tender to the touch and from the looks of all the blood on my fingers, it was bleeding like crazy. Head wounds always bleed huge amounts, though, even ones that aren't serious. I was *pretty* sure my ear was still firmly attached. Streghina looked into my eyes and smiled, my blood running down her chin and staining her teeth.

What a crazy fucked up bitch!

She ran toward me and wrapped her arms around me, our faces

just a few inches away from each other's. My sister locked gazes with me as we struggled against each other, and I couldn't free myself from her grip and push her away. She and I both knew that I was stronger than her, so why had she gotten in so close to me and wrapped her arms around me, like a lovers' embrace?

I'm not always the sharpest tool in the drawer; it took me a second to realize what she was doing. One critical second too long. By then it was too late: she was giving me what our mother, the Strega, had always called the *jettatura*, known to non-Sicilians as the Evil Eye.

My entire body starting feeling weak, my stomach nauseous, my legs wobbly. I dimly felt her let go of me and let me fall to the ground, but that might as well have been happening miles away for all the awareness or concern I had. My head was spinning and pounding, like no hangover I had ever experienced. My mouth flooded with saliva, and I was barely able to turn my head to one side before vomit poured out of my mouth and nose. It went on and on for what seemed like hours, but probably only lasted a minute or so. I just lay on the roof, my head back, my eyes closed, not hearing or feeling anything but the intense waves of cramps that coursed through my abdomen. My body tried to vomit up more, but there was just nothing left, so I suffered through bout after bout of dry heaves. I have no idea how long this all went on. It could have been minutes or hours. At various points I remember hoping, praying, that my sister would just kill me to put me out of my misery.

Eventually, the cramping and nausea diminished slightly, and I was able to muster up the strength to slowly shake my head from side to side, trying to clear it from the remnants of the *jettatura*. Eventually I was able to crawl to my hands and knees, which I viewed as one of the greatest achievements of my life. I stopped praying for death and began wishing I could just go home and fall into a coma. I sensed rather than saw something happening behind me. I rolled over and looked up into the sky. There was a hole there. Shit. Streghina must have been busy while I was out of it.

CHAPTER 16

I can't accurately describe what I glimpsed inside that rift in the sky. I wish I could, I really do, because then maybe I'd be able to stop thinking about it.

It assaulted my senses. In a way, what I saw reminded me vaguely of a jumble of sharp black spikes in that rift in the night sky, black on black, tangled together, but coupled with a sense of intelligence. Above all, what I sensed was evil. Evil beyond the petty cruelties we all encounter in our daily lives, evil beyond even what my mother and sister had done to my father and Jack. This was a kind of evil that wanted nothing more than to destroy, consume, annihilate anything and everything. There were discordant, jangling noises—I can't really even call them *sounds*—that seemed to seep into my bones and set my nerves on fire. There was a sense of unbelievably strong pressure from inside the rift, like that feeling you get just before a summer storm breaks, as well as a sense almost of *impatience* and, I have to say it, *hunger*. I could feel that whatever was in there desperately wanted out, and out *now*. Even though I was ten feet away, I could feel the pressure building and pressing against the rift, doing its damnedest to tear it wider. There was no way the containment pentagram my sister and the Fat Man had drawn could possibly contain it for much longer.

I couldn't stop staring at that rift. That's why I missed it when my sister ran over to me and knocked me off the roof of the cathedral.

I don't know where she got her strength from, but I couldn't prevent myself from getting flipped over the edge of the roof's two

119

foot high perimeter fence. I just barely managed to catch myself with both hands on the fence before I plummeted down a couple hundred feet. No way in hell I was going to look down to see my legs dangling over the edge into space, and I really didn't want my last sight to be my sister grinding my fingers under her shoes.

I hesitantly looked up, expecting to see her triumphant grin, and saw nothing. Hmm. She must have headed back to the rift in space to do something mystical and evil. Guess she was a little too distracted to finish me off just yet. I knew I might only have a minute or two before she rectified her mistake, plus—for obvious reasons—I wanted to get the hell back up onto the roof before my strength gave out.

My hands were sweaty, and I knew I was about to lose my grip, so I powered through the burning in my biceps and shoulders and scrambled back onto the roof and over the little fence as quietly as I could. I just lay there on my stomach for a second, my feet still hanging off the edge, just resting and trying to calm my hammering heart rate. Remind me never to fall off a roof again.

Eventually I was able to look up. My sister stood in the center of the roof, just staring into the void that was Tiamat, enraptured by whatever it was that she saw. I saw her lips moving, a string of drool hanging out of one corner of her mouth. It had her. It had her good.

I had no idea what to do to shut that rift in the sky, but I knew I had to do something. All I could think to do was to get my hands on that book. I looked around for it and saw it laying open on the roof, its pages turned to the last diagram, depicting a geometric shape more complex than any I had seen before. A finger of the rift in the sky seemed to bend down, pointing toward the center of that diagram, stopping just a few feet above the book.

I gathered my strength, took a deep breath, and ran over to the book, snatching it up and being ultra-careful to not come in contact with that rift. I still had to come within a few feet of it, and the cold coming out of the void seeped into my bones almost instantaneously. I stumbled and almost ate it, kicking the overturned hibachi and various mystic bullshit scattered around the book. I managed to keep my balance though, and slammed the book shut.

I heard a scream, a horrible, high-pitched wail of complete and under despair. It was so loud that it drove me to my knees, and my hands clenched over my ears did nothing to block it out. It was only a few seconds later that I realized the scream had not actually been heard in my ears, but had reverberated in my mind. All I know is, when that hole in the air shut with a thunderclap, I've never been so relieved in my entire life. The rift was gone. Thank God.

I looked up to see my sister standing there aghast, open-mouthed, staring at me. I struggled to my feet, grabbed her by the biceps, and started shaking her. "What in God's name were you even going to get Tiamat to do for you if you were successful in contacting it, Angela? What could possibly have been worth killing my partner and that guard downstairs and God knows who else?"

"What the fuck did you think I was going to do? Isn't it obvious?" she asked.

"No, not really, the whole concept is insane to me," even more so since I had seen a mere fraction of what Tiamat was.

"I was going to have it bring our mother back from the dead. And I was going to have you take her place in death."

"You know I should kill you for what you did to Jack and for what you just tried to do. You're too dangerous to live. You're like a rabid dog that just needs to be put down before it bites someone else."

"You can't kill me, you big pussy," she spat. "I'm your sister and deep down inside, you know you don't have the guts to kill me. You don't hate me enough."

I thought about that for what seemed to be a long time, but was probably only a couple seconds.

"No, you're right, Angela, I'm not going to kill you like I killed our mother." I have to admit, I enjoyed the look on her face when I spat that one out. "You aren't worth it to me. I'm going to let you live, but I'm going to make you wish you were dead. I'm going to give your True Name to every little pissant wizard in town who wants it, and they can steal all your power. If magic and power are all you care about, then that's what I'm going to take away from you, just like you took dad and Jack away from me. All your magic, all your power is going to dribble away as it's used up by every occult loser from here to Philly, Angela Maria Augustino."

Her jaw dropped, aghast. She opened and closed her mouth a couple times, trying to say something, but clearly not being able to get anything out. I didn't say a word, just looked at her, let her go.

Eventually she turned around and shuffled away. I half expected her to leap off the rooftop and fly away, or disappear in a cloud of brimstone, but she just slowly crawled down the ladder and went back into the cathedral.

I watched her walk away, then took stock of myself. My hands were numb from my sister's little electricity trick and hanging onto that fence for dear life, which was good because I knew that when the feeling returned, I was going to wish it hadn't. I could still feel the occasional small electric shock go through me. My entire body was one giant bruise, and I probably had a rib or three broken. My right ear was bleeding like crazy; I should probably get that stitched, or I'd end up looking like a pig with a notched ear. The back of my head was bleeding too, and I wasn't sure if I had a concussion. Both the Fat Man and Streghina were still alive, at least for now. I could always change that later. Jack was still dead though, and so was Little Boy. Not exactly a fair trade.

But I was alive.

And it felt great.

I grabbed the book from where it lay on the roof and headed back down the stairs.

CHAPTER 17

It took me a little while to find Jack's gun laying in the bushes where it had fallen off the roof. No way I was going to leave that sucker around for the police to find. I was still a little out of breath and not exactly feeling in tip-top condition by the time I made it back to the Bookworm's house. This had been a rough night for me—unless you lead a much more exciting life than I do, it's not often you're in two fights in one day where people are actively trying to kill you. I parked, did my damnedest to run up his sidewalk, and pushed aside the broken front door. The Bookworm and the Lector were both sitting in the living room on the couch facing the door. I was panting a little when I said, "I've got the book," and held it up so they—OK, so the Lector—could see it.

The Lector gave me the second smile I had ever seen cross her lips. Damn, that was almost worth what I had had to do to recover the damn book. Even the Bookworm smiled faintly. Not bad, considering what he had been through today. He looked a little better than when I had left.

"Did the doc ever come by to check on you, Bookworm?"

"He did. Can't say that was the best medical exam I've ever received, but he gave me some pain meds, and that's taking the edge off a little. Best of all, he didn't ask any questions. I didn't want to take so many painkillers that I wasn't lucid, though, just in case you did manage to recover the book."

"Just in case? Oh ye of little faith. You should have more confidence in me, Bookworm. Look, I need to rest for a minute, but let's get to it. I *really* want to not have to worry about this damn book anymore."

"Of course, Michael, have a seat. Take a load off. You're exactly right, now that we know so many people are interested in the book, it definitely needs to be destroyed tonight. Why don't you fill us in on what you've been up to since you left? What's going on with Fat Man and Streghina? Is there any danger they might come knocking any second to retrieve the book?"

I assured them there was no danger of that, while the Lector got me a glass of water, and I filled them in on what had transpired tonight. I figured we were all co-conspirators here, so I even told them I had had to kill Little Boy. Funny. I still didn't feel guilty about that one. I only got a twinge of guilt when I thought about the fact that Fat Man and my sister were probably still somewhere around the city. Hurt, and hurt badly (at least in the Fat Man's case), but still alive. I hoped I never came to regret not finishing them off when I had the chance. I told them both my sister's True Name. "So what do you think, Bookworm, can you drain her power, maybe to replace the mojo the Fat Man stole from you?"

He nodded grimly. "It's certainly worth a try. It won't be a perfect fit, but it should help a little anyway. But I'll deal with that in a day or two, once this is all over, and I've had a chance to recover a little."

I was ready to get to the heart of the matter. "So what do we have to do to finally destroy this stupid book? Can I just start ripping the pages out and setting them on fire? Got a lighter around here?"

"No, no, don't do that, Augustino. Definitely don't do that. There's a short destruction ritual we'll have to conduct. It's not like we can just destroy the book in a mundane fashion."

"Why the hell not? I'll be the first to admit I don't know much about magic, but this is basically just an ordinary book, right? It's just that it contains some very dangerous information. Right?"

"Well, no. Simple solutions won't work for this book, unfortunately. If we tried something like that, I'm afraid the book would attempt to defend itself. We could all easily die that way."

"Die? You mean, as in, the book could kill us? I've been slinging that thing all around the last couple of days, and it could have killed me?"

"No, no, only if you had tried to destroy the book. Otherwise, the book is perfectly content to remain quiescent and just sit there like any other book. It's not alive or even aware in any real sense, but it would know if it was about to be damaged or destroyed, and would take measures to prevent that from happening. What those measures are, well, I have no idea."

I really didn't like the sound of that and started grumbling.

The Bookworm took the hint and started telling the Lector what she needed to bring out to destroy the book. "Let's do it right here, in the living room. We're going to need some space to do this properly."

The Lector brought out an object that the Bookworm referred to as a "brazier." Apparently that means a big-ass metal bowl in a stand. Guess that's what wizards use for cook-outs. I helped her muscle it into the center of the room, and she spread some weird little pieces of wood in the bowl, while sprinkling them with random herbs and powders she pulled out of vials and pouches.

The Lector started to paint a pentagram or some other mystical geometric shape on the hardwood floor around the brazier. Man, the Bookworm was going to have to completely remodel his house after tonight.

That was when I looked up and saw all three members of the Triad standing in the doorway of the room.

Jesus Christ. I really didn't feel up to another fight tonight over this stupid book.

The woman I met earlier in the Flea Market parking lot was there, along with a woman who could easily have been her twin sister. The man they were with had short-cropped hair, where the women's hair was long, but otherwise, they looked like they had been cut from the same cloth. They were all wearing grey, loose-fitting, nondescript clothes. Absolutely nothing memorable about them. They were just standing there, hands at their sides.

One of the women started speaking. Same monotone as the last time I had heard her. Or maybe it was the other one. "Bookworm, the Triad has come for the book."

The man continued without missing a beat, "We have absolutely no interest in fighting you, nor do we lightly intrude upon you in your home."

The second woman: "But we must insist on taking possession of the book. We will do whatever is necessary to secure the book."

The Bookworm spoke up, facing in their general direction, a bloody bandage covering the ruins of his eyes. "We have never quarreled before, Triad. We have always peacefully co-existed. The book is mine now. We have gone to great trouble to acquire that book, risking our lives and paying great prices. None of our lives will ever be the same again because of that book. It has cost us too much. There is no way I can allow you to take the book. It is simply too dangerous to exist. Its potential for harm and destruction is too great."

One of the women replied, "There can be no compromise, Bookworm. We must have the book. We have plans for it."

The other woman said, "We will take the book from you if we have to, Bookworm. We cannot allow you to destroy the book. We need it." Interesting. Finally a hint of emotion. Her voice almost sounded plaintive.

This was going nowhere fast. They wanted the book, and we wouldn't let them have it without a fight. Mexican stand-off. The Lector and I had been ignored by the Triad to this point. All their attention was focused solely on the Bookworm. Jesus Christ. I just wanted to get a good night's sleep. That was going to have to wait a while though, I guess. I surreptitiously started to draw my flipknife out of my front pocket. Like that would do much good.

The Lector said, "Enough is enough," blew air into her cheeks and exhaled at them, like she was blowing an invisible trumpet.

It looked like all three members of the Triad were caught up in a hurricane. There appeared to be gale force winds blowing right at them and pushing them back out the front door. They fought it as best they could, but eventually, no one could stand in the face of that much wind, and they were knocked to the floor. They started to skid backward across the hardwood floor. They tried to clutch at various pieces of furniture as they skidded by, but they just couldn't hold on long enough.

Once all three of them had been pushed out the front door, sprawling onto the front porch, the Lector stopped exhaling, and the wind died instantly. She made a gesture and the front door slammed shut and locked, despite the fact that it had been off its hinges. It looked like the door and the front windows had a soft amber glow. I was guessing that it wouldn't be a good idea for the Triad to come back in through the doors or windows of the house. If the look on the Lector's face was any indication, I suspected that would be a *very* bad idea.

"How the hell did you do that? You on magical steroids?"

"I wasn't going to take any chances. We're too close to finishing this damn thing off."

"Fair enough. Just didn't know you had it in you."

The Bookworm piped up. "Oh she's very impressive, Augustino. Never underestimate the Lector's abilities. She will surprise you every time." He hadn't moved an inch on the couch, though he now had a broad smile on his face.

Wow. The Lector was a heavy hitter herself. Who knew?

CHAPTER 18

"All right," the Bookworm said. "We've wasted enough time. Let me have the book for a moment." I walked over and put it in his hands.

The Bookworm was quiet for a minute, just running his hands over the book's cover, then idly flipping through its pages. The way his head was tilted toward it, I could have sworn he was staring at it as he turned the pages, though I knew he couldn't be. Not having eyes anymore, and all. "Lector, Augustino, what do you think? The book actually presents a tremendous opportunity. Rather than contacting Tiamat and asking for power, or glory, or whatever it was that the Fat Man or Augustino's sister were going to ask for, we could actually ask it to reshape the world for the better. I mean, think about it, we have in our hands the means to change the world. Make the world the best possible place it can be. No more evil, no more death, or wars, or sickness . . . ."

That made me nervous as shit. We couldn't afford to have the Bookworm go wobbly on us now. We needed his knowledge if we were ever going to get rid of this goddamned book.

"No way, no how, Bookworm. You can't honestly believe that Tiamat could be persuaded to make the world a better place. If even half the stuff you've told me about that thing is true, we can't trust it not to destroy us, and maybe the rest of the world as soon as we've let it into our dimension. Besides, you guys didn't see that rift that my sister and the Fat Man opened. I did. I saw a glimpse of Tiamat. I saw and felt and heard and smelled what that thing is really like.

That thing is *pure evil.* No way it's going to make the world all sweetness and light, just because you ask it pretty please. It just wants to destroy."

"He's right," the Lector chimed in. "You know how dangerous Tiamat is, Bookworm. It doesn't want to help its summoners. I'm not even sure it can be bargained with. It's simply evil, evil of a type unfathomable by mere humans like us. There's no way it would actually *help* us. Can't you see that?"

The Bookworm's face looked anguished. "Take it, take it!" He held the book out in his outstretched hands, as if to get it as far away from himself as possible. The Lector took a quick stride over to him and snatched it away, clutching it against her chest.

The Bookworm didn't say anything for a long while, and neither did we. "I'm sorry . . . . I'm very sorry. I don't know what came over me. You're right, of course, the book has to be destroyed. I know that. I *know* that." I couldn't tell if he was trying to convince himself or us.

"That's OK, Bookworm, ol' buddy. Let's just get this thing destroyed. The sooner, the better, right?"

"You're right, you're right, Augustino. I'm sorry, both of you. I don't know what came over me. I'm fine now though. Everything's fine."

The Bookworm and the Lector started discussing the ritual. It sounded like the Lector was going to be pretty much on her own with this one. The Bookworm wasn't in the best shape to be casting spells at this point. Not that I minded much. After seeing the "Last Temptation of the Bookworm" just now, I wasn't entirely sure he could be trusted to destroy the book on his own. I'm guessing the Lector had similar suspicions, since she didn't let go of the book the entire time they were talking. Plus, after seeing what happened to the Triad, she clearly had the raw power required.

They talked for five or ten minutes about ritual minutiae. I didn't understand more than the occasional verb. Let's hope the Lector had all that down pat.

The Lector placed the book down on a small table I dragged over for her. Clearly, she was going to need both hands for this. She finished drawing the pentagram, then stood in front of the brazier, her head bowed and book in hand. The ritual had begun in earnest.

The Lector began to chant, periodically making ritualistic gestures and throwing various substances in the brazier. I have no idea what most of them were, but I can testify that they created really bizarre smelling smoke (and not in a good way) and sometimes caused colored flames to flare up. While I was watching the Lector, I heard a slight rustling sound and looked down at the book. Something was going on with it. It was kind of vibrating. After a couple seconds, the cover flew open with a snap, and the pages started turning.

I was reluctant to disturb the Lector mid-spell, but I had to ask, "Um, is that supposed to be happening?"

She stopped after a second, looked down at the book. "No. No, it's not."

The pages had stopped turning when they reached a spot about halfway through the book. A thin gray smoke started coming from the center of the book, but it wasn't on fire though, I could see that much.

I figured I might as well get an expert opinion before I completely panicked. Besides, it's not like the blind guy was doing anything important right now. "Bookworm, the book opened by itself, and now there's gray smoke coming up from it! But we haven't set it on fire yet though. What the hell is going on?"

"Oh shit!" he said. I hate it when wizards say that. "The book can sense that we're trying to destroy it. Its defenses are probably summoning some kind of spirit. What does it look like?"

I had to squint for a minute, but the smoke was coalescing and beginning to take on a more coherent form. The spirit materializing in the center of the room was someone a lot more imposing than the illusion of the old Jewish lady—Mort's wife—I had seen all those many years ago with Jack. This time, I knew it wasn't the illusionary conjuring of a second-rate hack. This was the real deal. A real, honest-to-God, incredibly pissed off looking Ben Franklin from beyond the grave, looking just like I had imagined he would look. And from the looks of the smoky forms taking shape behind him, ol' Ben had brought some of his dead Masonic brethren with him.

Oh shit indeed.

The Lector described what we were seeing to the Bookworm. He shakily rose from the couch and said, "Lector, use the Third Rite of Exorcism, it's the only way we can be sure!" Whatever. Sounded good to me (not that I knew what he was talking about), at least someone around here had a plan.

The Lector nodded her head and seemed to spring into action. "We need a bell, my book of exorcisms, and a candle, quick! I'll grab the book myself. Augustino, you find a bell and a candle in that bag of ritual items." She pointed to a large, brown leather bag half-open against the far wall. "Whatever you do, Augustino, you've got to get that book shut after I complete the ritual chant, ring the bell, and extinguish the candle."

I made sure that good ol' Ben and his buddies were still busy materializing over the book (they were, though they were looking more and more solid—and angry—and three-dimensional by the second), then I scrambled to find a bell and a candle. It took me way longer to find them in that mess of a bag than I wanted, but eventually I came across the desired items and handed them off to the Lector. She immediately began chanting in Latin, reading from her book. I hung back a little, since it looked to me like the ghosts were starting to get way more pissed off than I wanted to deal with.

The Lector continued her chant in a loud, firm voice. I was impressed. After all we had been through today, I was almost in awe that she wasn't lying under the couch in a fetal position. The exorcism ritual looked (to me, a know-nothing layman) like it was holding the ghosts at bay. They weren't happy by any means, but they weren't ripping our hearts out yet either, despite the fact that Ben and company were almost as real-looking as the Lector and the Bookworm. I took that as a good sign. After a minute or so of the chant, the Lector tapped the side of the bell with a metal striker, and its peal seemed to echo throughout the room, far louder than the small bell should have been capable of producing. Franklin and the Masonic ghosts threw back their heads, clasped their hands over their ears and howled, the sound of it inaudible over the sound of the bell's ringing. The Lector lifted the candle and blew it out with a quick puff. The entire room dimmed, and shadows danced along the walls and ceiling, almost seeming to converge on us.

I knew it was my turn, now or never.

I grabbed a hold of the book with both hands and immediately felt resistance. Which was weird, since it was just a book, right? There hadn't been any resistance when I shut the door in the sky over the roof of the National Cathedral. I got a better grip on the cover and put my back into it, grunting and heaving to get that bastard shut.

I looked up and almost shat myself because Ben Franklin's specter was reaching down toward me, the nails on his hand long and ragged. His mouth was frozen in a rictus, and his eyes were black depths, staring into my own. Just as I began to feel his icy touch on my hand, the book finally shut with a clap, but the feel of frostbite and biting cold lingered for a second. The ghosts were gone, the book shut.

"Lector, hurry up and burn this fucker!"

She snatched the book away from me and threw it in the still-burning brazier. It started to catch fire around the edges, but not fast enough for her, because she squirted a bottle of lighter fluid on top of it. The flames sprang up, all blues and greens and purples, casting obscene shadows halfway to the ceiling, but the book was getting crispier by the second. We couldn't help but just stare into the flames, watching the book that had caused so much pain being destroyed.

Eventually the book was just a pile of dark ash, consumed by the flames. At least the flames had returned to normal colors, and there were no longer specters of long-dead Freemasons flying around the room. I felt everyone breathe a big sigh of relief—I know I did. The Bookworm sat back down on the couch, the Lector walking over to him.

I ran over to open the windows to let some of the oily smoke out of the room. The Bookworm was in serious need of a remodeling crew for his house. I righted an overturned easy chair and plopped down so I could catch my breath.

Now I just had to get my check for twenty grand from the Bookworm and break the news to him that he needed to come up with a half a truckload full of Spam in exchange for the book or he was going to have a pack of very angry—and hungry—Munchkins on his hands . . . .

EPILOGUE

When I got back from the Flea Market, Sarah was sitting on the couch, smoking and watching TV. She had hardly left my couch in the weeks she had been living with me. The apartment stunk of cigarettes, dirty food plates, and body odor. She wasn't taking care of herself and had more or less given up hope. I can only imagine what it must have been like to be a tall, beautiful, desirable woman who had been reduced to her current short, dumpy, ugly state.

"Sarah, I don't want to get your hopes up, but I picked up something for you. It might help."

"What do you mean?" she said, barely looking up from the sitcom she was watching.

"Well, I picked you up this special cream that—"

"You've gotta be fucking kidding me! There's no way some stupid cream is going to help me. Look at me! I'm *ugly*!" She started sobbing. Sarah had been crying almost non-stop since I found her. At least she was alive. And not catatonic, like I was afraid she might turn out to be.

I tried to comfort her as best as I could, but what could I really say? She had been tall and beautiful before the Munchkins took her, and now she really *was* ugly. "Look, will you try this for me? It's not some kind of store-bought crap. It's well, special . . . please? It cost me a lot." I didn't want to think about what I had to offer the old lady at the Flea Market for this cream.

"Ok, OK, I'll try it," she finally mumbled. "It can't make me any worse, can it?" She tried to smile through the tears, but it was a real

133

effort.

"Look, Sarah . . . before you try this stuff, I need to be honest with you. It's not going to make you beautiful again. I . . . I don't know of any magic powerful enough to restore your old appearance. It may be out there, but I don't know what it would entail or how to find it. This stuff . . . well, the lady I got it from said that it would make you average looking. Not great looking. Not anyone who would ever turn heads, or have guys on the street look at you twice. You'd just be . . . *average*."

She thought about it a long, long time. "Fuck it," she said through silent tears. "Let's do it. Looking average is better than nothing. I guess. I'm a freak. I can't even leave the apartment looking like this. I don't care if I can't dance any more, but I don't want to be a monster. Do it!"

I helped her rub the stuff all over her face, making sure she didn't miss any spots. It smelled like some strange mix of spices and scents I couldn't identify. By the time we finished, she was pretty lethargic and seemed on the verge of falling asleep. I laid her out on the couch, then proceeded to rub her down completely, making sure the cream covered her arms, legs, breasts, and back, just like the old lady told me. Sarah was completely knocked out by the time I finished, so I just let her sleep it off on the couch, crossed my fingers, and waited.

#

Sarah woke up a day and a half later. She was more than a little groggy at first, but when she looked in the mirror I handed her, she became instantly alert.

She didn't say anything. Just stared and stared at herself. Touched her face all over. She was, well, just average-looking. 5'6", mouse-brown hair, plain brown eyes, small-ish breasts, not fat but not thin either. Not anyone you'd ever look at twice, or even notice. She looked like a grocery store clerk or something. Eventually, she looked at me. Gave me a little smile that broke a piece of my heart off and stepped on it. "I'll never have what I used to have before, will I?"

I couldn't answer her, couldn't get the words out, couldn't even look at her. I couldn't make up my mind if I had done her a favor or not.

But everything was going to be all right. For Sarah, for me, for the Bookworm and the Lector. Right? Oh, hell. You and I both know that isn't true. Besides, if things were fine, why did I still have nightmares every night?

# # #

ACKNOWLEDGMENTS AND AUTHOR'S NOTES

I began writing this one in January 2006. Most of it was finished by the end of February 2006, but I put the finishing touches on it that August. Then the manuscript sat and sat before I decided to dust it off, polish it up, and see if I could get it published. In the interim, I realized that a terrible thing had happened: they decided to physically *move* "The Awakening" statue out of Hains Point and into the National Harbor in Prince George's County, Maryland in 2008. That crushed my soul. Alas. If that bugs you, just assume the present-day parts of the story are set in January 2006. Check it out at its new home, it's an amazing piece of sculpture and I have by no means done justice in my treatment of it here. I've also moved the roof entrance of the National Cathedral slightly, since I figured its custodians probably wouldn't appreciate me telling random sorcerers and ne'er-do-wells how to get onto the roof. But do take the tour of that too the next time you're in town. Everything else is as real as I could make it, subject to my very subjective assessments as a long-time DC area resident. I suspect that since 2006, the Flea Market has likely had to move a couple times due to the gentrification in the city, but *c'est la vie*.

The novel would not have happened had it not been for some very good friends who have supported my writing and other endeavors over the years, including my wife, and good friends Scott, Megan, and Chad. Francesca was also very helpful years ago when I needed a Sicilian to bounce a few ideas off.

Please see my personal website at http://ryanrennik.com/ and my publisher's website at http://uncannybooks.com/

I am working on a sequel to *As Above, So Below* as well as a few other novels I think you'll enjoy.

ABOUT THE AUTHOR

Ryan Rennik is the pseudonym of a published author who has lived in the Washington, DC area for more than a decade. *As Above, So Below* is the first novel in the Augustino Case Files series as well as his first novel as Ryan Rennik.

www.ingramcontent.com/pod-product-compliance
Lightning Source LLC
Chambersburg PA
CBHW060741180626
46819CB00001B/58